-THE CHRONICLES OF-
NARNIA

THE LION, THE WITCH AND THE WARDROBE

THE OFFICIAL ILLUSTRATED
MOVIE COMPANION

PERRY MOORE

Executive Producer of *The Chronicles of Narnia*

HarperSanFrancisco
A Division of HarperCollins*Publishers*

THE CHRONICLES OF NARNIA:
THE LION, THE WITCH AND THE WARDROBE

WALT DISNEY PICTURES AND WALDEN MEDIA PRESENT "THE CHRONICLES OF NARNIA: THE LION, THE WITCH AND THE WARDROBE" BASED ON THE BOOK BY C.S. LEWIS A MARK JOHNSON PRODUCTION AN ANDREW ADAMSON FILM MUSIC COMPOSED BY HARRY GREGSON-WILLIAMS COSTUME DESIGNER ISIS MUSSENDEN EDITED BY SIM EVAN-JONES PRODUCTION DESIGNER ROGER FORD DIRECTOR OF PHOTOGRAPHY DONALD M. McALPINE, ASC, ACS CO-PRODUCER DOUGLAS GRESHAM EXECUTIVE PRODUCERS PHILIP STEUER ANDREW ADAMSON PERRY MOORE SCREENPLAY BY ANN PEACOCK AND ANDREW ADAMSON AND CHRISTOPHER MARKUS & STEPHEN McFEELY PRODUCED BY MARK JOHNSON DIRECTED BY ANDREW ADAMSON

Narnia.com

FIRST EDITION

Designed by Joel Avirom, Jason Snyder, and Meghan Day Healey

Library of Congress Cataloging-in-Publication Data is available.

ISBN-10: 0–06–082787–4

ISBN-13: 978–0–06–082787–8

05 06 07 08 09 RRD(W) 10 9 8 7 6 5 4 3 2 1

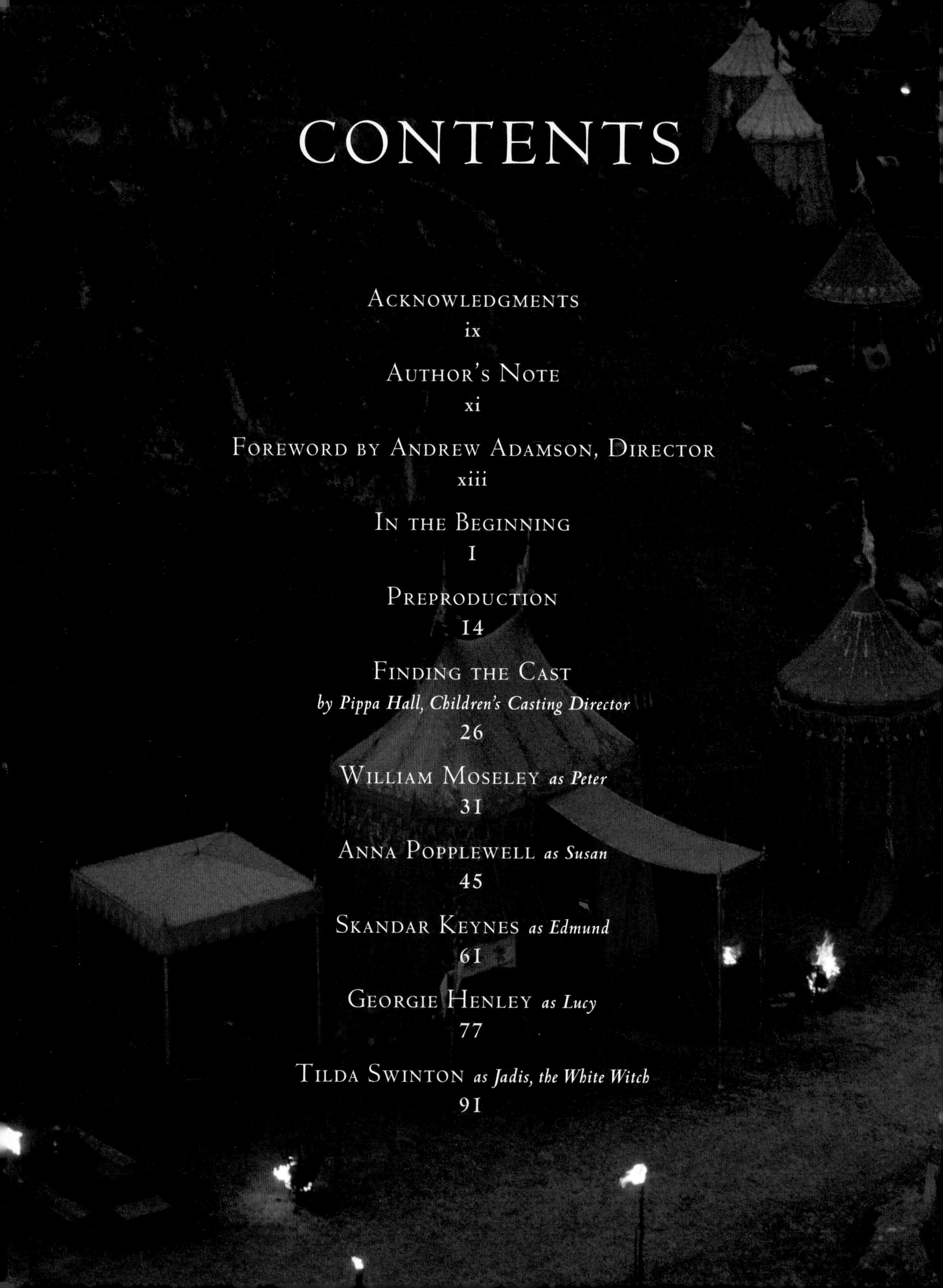

CONTENTS

ACKNOWLEDGMENTS
ix

AUTHOR'S NOTE
xi

FOREWORD BY ANDREW ADAMSON, DIRECTOR
xiii

IN THE BEGINNING
1

PREPRODUCTION
14

FINDING THE CAST
by Pippa Hall, Children's Casting Director
26

WILLIAM MOSELEY *as Peter*
31

ANNA POPPLEWELL *as Susan*
45

SKANDAR KEYNES *as Edmund*
61

GEORGIE HENLEY *as Lucy*
77

TILDA SWINTON *as Jadis, the White Witch*
91

ANNA'S JOURNAL: A NARNIA DIARY
104

GEORGIE'S INTERVIEWS: GOING BEHIND THE SCENES
114

AN EPIC CHALLENGE: AN INTERVIEW WITH ANDREW ADAMSON
123

MAKING NARNIA A REAL PLACE:
ROGER FORD AND THE PRODUCTION DESIGN TEAM
137

THE WONDERFUL WORLD OF WETA
by Ben Wootten, Richard Taylor, and Weta Workshop
153

CREATURE FEATURE: NARNIA'S TALKING BEASTS
by Howard Berger, Head Creature Designer and Supervisor
163

REAL MAGIC: CREATING THE SPECIAL EFFECTS OF NARNIA
by Dean Wright, Supervisor of Visual Effects
181

THE COSTUMES OF NARNIA:
PUTTING THE WARDROBE INTO THE WARDROBE
201

WHAT IT ALL MEANS:
AN INTERVIEW WITH DOUGLAS GRESHAM, C. S. LEWIS'S STEPSON
211

WE'LL ALWAYS HAVE PRAGUE: THE FINAL DAYS OF SHOOTING
222

A DREAM COMES TRUE: AN AFTERWORD BY DOUGLAS GRESHAM
224

ACKNOWLEDGMENTS

*The author wishes to thank the following people, without whose help and guidance
this book would never have been possible.*

Hunter Hill
Andrew Adamson
Douglas and Merrie Gresham
Phil Anschutz
Cary Granat
Micheal Flaherty
Doreen Do
Ernie Malik
Joel Avirom
Jason Snyder
Meghan Day Healey
Mickey Maudlin
Terri Leonard
Cynthia DiTiberio
Claudia Boutote
Toni Markiet
Mark Johnson
Philip Steuer
Tom Williams
Mark Simone
Alina Phelan
Melvin Adams
Rudi Sieber
Simon Adley
Christine Cadena
Dennis Rice
John Sable
Tilda Swinton
William Moseley
Georgie Henley
Helen and Mike Henley

Peter and Julie Moseley
Skandar Keynes
Zelfa Hourani and Randall Keynes
Anna Popplewell
Debra Lomas and Andrew Popplewell
James McAvoy
Richard Taylor
Ben Wootten
Howard Berger
Dean Wright
Don McAlpine
Sim Evan-Jones
Pippa Hall
Gail Stevens
Rpin Suwannath
Randy Starr
Justin Sweet
Roger Ford
Isis Mussenden
Slab
Beth DePatie
Tim Coddington
Hope Atherton
Kiran Shah
Shane Rangi
Patrick Kake
Ralph Brescia
Allison Sarofim
Lauren Levine
Henrik Tamm
Mary McAveney

And a special thanks to my mother, Nancy Moore,
for giving me the book when I was a boy and starting this whole thing.

AUTHOR'S NOTE

By Perry Moore

This book is meant to be a keepsake for fans of the new Narnia movie, fans of the book, and fans of the story. It's a little out of the ordinary for a producer to write a making-of-the-movie book, but I agreed to it because I wanted to share this incredible journey with others. I think fans deserve something more personal than some press notes cobbled together with publicity photos. This book will be a little more personal, written from the perspective of someone who was there, someone who was proud to be a part of it all.

The story of how this movie came to be is as remarkable as the tale itself. For those of you who love The Lion, the Witch and the Wardrobe *as much as I do, I hope you'll treasure this book as a special companion piece to the greatest story ever told.*

FOREWORD

By Andrew Adamson, Director

I WAS ABOUT EIGHT YEARS OLD WHEN MY parents gave me *The Lion, the Witch and the Wardrobe.* I lost myself in C. S. Lewis's magical world of mythical creatures, talking animals, and childhood wonder. As I continued to read all of the books in the Narnia Chronicles, the world and the characters that inhabit it expanded to fill my imagination. I could hardly dream then that I would one day be drawing on that childhood imagination to bring this world to the screen.

It is not everyone who gets the chance to bring childhood dreams to life and it was a task that I did not undertake lightly. For those of us who were brought up with these stories it was vital that the movie live up to the world C. S. Lewis had created. This might not have been possible only a few years ago, but the many recent advances in filmmaking technology have allowed this story finally to be told.

Making a movie of this scope is akin to mounting an army, a giant machine with all its pieces working in unison. It would take an incredible team of caring craftspeople, writers, producers, actors, cinematographers, assistant directors, editors, composers, designers, illustrators, camera operators, set decorators, costume designers, production managers, grips, electricians, caterers, drivers, stunt performers, sound recordists, sound designers, visual effects artists, video assist operators, cable handlers, animal handlers, talent handlers, assistants, assistants to assistants . . . and on and on. These are the people to whom I will be eternally grateful for bringing my eight-year-old imagination to life.

The story behind the making of *The Lion, the Witch and the Wardrobe* is as rich in detail and as populated with characters as the world of Narnia itself. This is a book about those people. A story of camaraderie, courage, frustration, tears, blood, sweat, and caring—the story of the journey we all took to bring you this film.

June 2005

IN THE BEGINNING

IT TAKES NOTHING SHORT OF A MIRACLE to make a movie. There are a vast number of moving targets that have to line up in order to get a film going—the scheduling, the budget, the multitudes of people involved, the rights, the studio, the cast, the director, the vision. It takes an even bigger miracle to make a good movie.

This is the story of that miracle.

From my point of view, like millions of other children, the story begins in the library. My mother took my sister and me to the library once a week like clockwork, and each week I'd come home with a new book to explore. At first it was Dr. Seuss or the like — picture books, mostly. Then one day my mother handed me a book with more words than pictures.

I looked down at the title: *The Lion, the Witch and the Wardrobe.* It was the first book I read that topped a hundred pages, and I was hooked on the story from page one. Narnia, a seemingly endless land where magic prevailed and the good guys vanquished the forces of evil, was a part of me from that moment on. I started dreaming about it then, and to be honest, I've

never stopped. It wasn't uncommon for Mom to find me checking the back walls of pantries, linen closets, and dressing rooms, all to no avail. One day, when we went to buy a new couch for the den, I went missing. My parents enlisted the security guards, who finally found me in the warehouse, knocking on the back of a wardrobe. On the way home, I laid my head against the car window and scanned the fields and forest for Centaurs and Fauns and Dwarfs.

A few years went by. School. College and a degree in English literature. Some entry-level jobs in film and television—some good, some bad. A long, hard haul up the ladder. Then one day I found myself in what I now call "the right place at the right time."

I joined a company called Walden Media, where my job was to find movie projects that fit the company's mandate. The heads of the company, CEO Cary Granat and president Micheal Flaherty, had set up a film studio devoted to making quality films with educational merit. The man who financed our company, Philip Anschutz, was a self-made billionaire from

Denver and a man with a mission: he wanted to make quality movies that would inspire viewers to make the world a better place.

An excellent mission by all accounts. I'd made a list of all my favorite books from school reading lists. Though I periodically edited the list, one book always remained in the number-one spot: *The Lion, the Witch and the Wardrobe*. Fortunately, I found that I had an ally at the company in Micheal Flaherty, who also shared my love for this property since childhood. In fact, when Micheal and Cary had first approached Phil Anschutz with the idea to invest in their new company the year before, *The Lion, the Witch and the Wardrobe* was the most important property they described when they presented him with a vision of the types of films they hoped to create. In my previous job, I'd learned that another Hollywood studio had purchased an option to make the film.

Still, I'm a firm believer in positive thinking. Sometimes you literally have to *will* a movie into existence. So I called someone I knew at that studio, who had no idea that they even owned the rights to Narnia. Not a great sign that they had any intention of making the movie. I did a little more investigating and found out that there had been plans to update the story, setting it in modern-day Los Angeles after an earthquake rather than in London during the Blitz. The Turkish Delight that I'd found so exotic and intriguing as a child threatened to go out the window in favor of hot dogs and cheeseburgers.

I made a vow then and there: this story had to be done right, and that meant being faithful to the book.

A little more research taught me that it was the C. S. Lewis Company (in effect, Lewis's estate) to whom we should make our pitch. We knew they believed, as did we at Walden Media, that the movie needed to remain faithful to the book.

I'd also learned it's not uncommon for movie rights to revert after a certain period of time if there's no intention of making the movie. Since the studio I'd spoken with didn't even know they owned the book, it seemed likely that the rights would revert one day.

Our pitch to the C. S. Lewis Company had to be inspired, sincere, and responsible. But I knew I loved this book more than anything, and was confident that Walden Media could get it made the right way. That was the essence of my pitch.

I tracked down the C. S. Lewis Company and sent them a well-intentioned letter that expressed Walden Media's belief in the power of the property and requested an introductory meeting the next time they found themselves in New York. I got an immediate response from Melvin Adams, the organization's managing director, who said he came to New York periodically to meet with their publisher, Harper Collins. As luck would have it, he was going to be in New York in a month, and so we scheduled a breakfast meeting at his hotel.

The day before the meeting, I was printing out my notes, and as I walked by the conference room I bumped into a man strolling down the hallway with Walden Media's Cary Granat and Mike Flaherty.

"Perry, I'd like you to meet Phil Anschutz," Micheal said. "Perry is pursuing a very important property for us."

Phil shook my hand and asked how things were going. It wasn't a perfunctory question. He was genuinely interested.

"So, Perry," Phil said, "what are you working on?"

I looked down at the presentation in my hand.

"Actually, I have a meeting tomorrow with the head of the C. S. Lewis estate. I'm going to convince him to give us the rights to make a movie version of *The Lion, the Witch and the Wardrobe.*"

A beat went by and no one said anything. Unlike most successful businessmen, Phil is not a man of too many words. He's more a man who sticks by his words. I looked over nervously at Cary and Mike.

Then Phil spoke.

"I would be very, very much interested in that project," he said with a smile.

I showed up at the hotel on the appointed day, arriving half an hour early to review my pitch one last time. I looked at the notes for a few minutes and then decided I knew them well enough. I wanted our meeting to sound like it was coming from my heart. I called up to Melvin's room, and he told me he'd be right down. I pitched my heart out, promising to make a faithful adaptation of the book we all loved. When Melvin and I shook hands a couple of hours later, we had agreed to continue talking. But it would take almost a full year of creative discussions and negotiations by the whole Walden Media team before the rights would officially be granted.

During that year two blockbuster movies came out: *Harry Potter and the Sorcerer's Stone* and *The Lord of the Rings: The Fellowship of the Ring.* In November 2001 Harry Potter took life on screens worldwide, and to no one's surprise that picture rewrote box-office history. The surprise to come was that *The Lord of the Rings,* when it came out shortly thereafter, would rewrite box-office history, too.

What this meant for us was that fantasy films were back in fashion, bigger and better than ever. The almighty dollar had spoken, and Hollywood took note. The result was that every studio and production company now

stepped forward and approached the Lewis estate aggressively for the movie rights to Narnia. There was only one major fantasy franchise left of the magnitude and renown of *Harry Potter* and *The Lord of the Rings:* the Narnia Chronicles.

My stomach dropped on any number of occasions that final week of negotiations. Loyal to a fault, the Lewis estate respected and appreciated our early interest in the books. They also liked our vision for the film, a faithful adaptation with them on board as our partner. But other studios were on the phone routinely, lobbying heavily with last-minute entreaties for the film rights. Had we come this far only to lose out in a bidding war?

We sat down with each other face-to-face in New York for the final negotiations. Phil Anschutz arrived and met Douglas Gresham, stepson of C. S. Lewis and the heart and soul of the estate, the man who protects the integrity of Lewis's works as the company's creative director. It turned out to be a momentous occasion, a meeting that would seal the deal for good. In that meeting, we promised to be faithful to the story. We talked about how we would make a film of the scale and epic quality of *The Lord of the Rings.*

Phil thanked Gresham and his associates for coming, asked them to outline what they thought was a fair deal for the rights, and listened attentively to their presentation. Not one for protracted negotiations, Phil closed the deal in a matter of minutes.

About a month later, over a 3 A.M. toast at the Chewton Glen Hotel near Lymington, England, we signed the paperwork confirming our partnership to make a faithful adaptation of *The Lion, the Witch and the Wardrobe.*

The real work had just begun. Now we had to make the movie.

ENTER THE DIRECTOR

An amazing movie demands an equally amazing director. Film is a director's medium. Anyone who doesn't believe that, try to imagine how *The Lord of the Rings* would have been made without Peter Jackson.

We had the crown jewel of all movie material in *The Lion, the Witch and the Wardrobe.* Now we needed the best of the best to direct it—someone with a vision as pure and inspired as the one guiding the book itself.

There were plenty of incredibly talented people interested in the project, but months passed and still we had no director. There hadn't been that moment yet, that magical instant where you know someone is the right person beyond a shadow of a doubt.

And then that magical moment came when Cary and I went to meet with Andrew Adamson one morning.

He was wary about what we wanted to do with the movie. Andrew made it clear that he wanted to make a movie that would be a faithful adaptation of his memory of the book. *The Lion, the Witch and the Wardrobe* had occupied a special place in his own imagination, and it was that experience he was interested in recreating.

Andrew explained that when he reread *The Chronicles of Narnia* as an adult, he was surprised at how small some of the action was on the page. For instance, his childhood memory of "a huge, vivid battle of good and evil with a whole menagerie of mythological creatures" turned out to last little more than a page in the book. "It's Peter basically telling Aslan what happened in retrospect," Andrew said, "but I remembered it as this incredible battle with Minotaurs against Centaurs against Fauns and Satyrs—different creatures against different creatures, each with its own special skill. A Phoenix can flame up and catch light. A Minotaur can fight with weapons but also with horns. So you get a whole new form of battle."

As Andrew pointed out, "C. S. Lewis wrote in a way that was very minimalist. Unlike Tolkien, who spelled everything out and was very specific,

---

BELOW: *Conceptual illustration of the children arriving at Aslan's camp.*

OPPOSITE: *Director Andrew Adamson.*

NEXT PAGES: *Conceptual art for the battle.*

C. S. Lewis painted a picture and left a lot to one's imagination. Our challenge is to bring the film to the level of imagination Lewis inspired." If we were up for that challenge, Andrew told us, then he was our director. If not, it had been nice meeting us.

Cary and I both knew we'd met our man. A few days later our impression was confirmed. Out of the blue Andrew called to say he'd had a little think about the film over the weekend and wanted to send us some thoughts. What came through the fax machine surprised me.

Andrew had compiled twenty pages of detailed notes, providing a broad overview of the movie he wanted to make. What's remarkable is that so many of the ideas on that list of rough notes have prevailed. He listed his thoughts on casting, the evolution of each child's character, possible settings, music, how to flesh out the narrative for the big screen, everything you could possibly think of concerning a movie this epic. He even charted the progress of the movie's color palette—opening up with muted grays for the initial London bombing sequences, working through cold icy blues and whites during the

ABOVE: *Author Clive Staples Lewis; "Jack" to those who knew him.*

BELOW: *Tumnus's home in the Czech Republic.*

OPPOSITE: *Spring blossoms in Narnia.*

White Witch's winter-locked Narnia sequences, and finally exploding with colors as Aslan and spring burst into Narnia.

Andrew's vision, even in these earliest thoughts, was breathtaking. We had our director.

Now we had to approach our partners, the C. S. Lewis Company, with the news. They liked the idea of bringing a fresh talent to a classic project and were eager to meet Andrew. We flew him to New York one day to introduce him. It didn't take long for him to impress the estate. "He's a genius," Doug Gresham said. "He is to my mind the only man to do the job today . . . the only director for this project."

Plus, Doug added, Andrew would have to play Puddleglum when we got around to making *The Silver Chair*, a later book in *The Chronicles of Narnia*. He's the spitting image of Puddleglum the Marshwiggle, Doug told us.

We gave Andrew two gifts, tokens of our faith in his ability to lead the movie: a bullwhip and a bottle of catnip, symbols of our faith that he'd be able to tame any problems he encountered along the way (with lions or otherwise). The gifts created a problem of their own: they caused no small commotion at the airport, where the security screeners stopped him as he tried to board his return flight. They'd spotted something on the X ray.

"Sir, can you open your bag, please?" the security guard asked Andrew in front of a long line of testy passengers.

Andrew unzipped his bag, hesitated, and pulled out a giant bullwhip and a bottle of catnip (which bears an uncanny resemblance to a certain illicit substance for those of you who've never seen it). The people in line behind Andrew snickered. The security guards smirked. Andrew tried to explain he'd just gotten this great job to direct a movie, and it starred a lion and—

"It's okay," the security guard grinned. "Go ahead."

There would be a thousand more obstacles for Andrew to overcome to make the movie. I've often wondered if Andrew ever thought to himself, "What on earth have I gotten myself into?"

PRE-PREPRODUCTION

Most films have a few months of set-up time, officially known as preproduction. In our case, in order to create an entire world that lived inside the imagination, we needed a little more time.

We had to create an entire, believable world before we could shoot a single frame of film. "To me, Narnia is a real place," Andrew explained. "Lucy goes through a wardrobe and steps into a world that has to be believable." Okay, easy enough. Now not only do we have to make a movie that lives up to our director's imagining of it as a child, but that world has to be 100 percent believable.

"I think the most daunting thing is the responsibility to a beloved readership," Andrew said. "These books have been read by hundreds of millions of people over three or four generations, and those people all have an image in their mind of what Narnia is. And it's a huge responsibility to be making a film that's going to live up to those people's expectations."

Where would we start? Well, one of the very first things Andrew did was hire a team of the most talented artists in the world to begin rendering the literary world in purely visual terms.

Andrew had known the fine folks at New Zealand's Weta Workshop for years. This was the same ragtag crew that had been responsible for the massive prosthetics, makeup, and creature effects for *The Lord of the Rings*. We brought them on immediately to begin conceptual illustration. We also assembled a staff of wildly talented artists in a production office in Los Angeles, working around the clock on defining the look and feel of the movie.

Conceptual art of Lucy meeting Tumnus in Narnia.

Sometimes we managed to convene all the artists and filmmakers in the same room at the same time, and the results could be magic. Take, for instance, the translation of Father Christmas from page to screen.

It would be pretty easy to argue that Father Christmas's brief appearance in the book is a little strange. The kids are in this magical otherworld, and yet they have our Santa Claus? One solution would have been to do away with Father Christmas altogether and have Aslan give the kids their gifts at his camp instead. Yet because Andrew was committed to remaining faithful to the book, he was determined to come up with a solution.

As we sat around a table in our conference room—the team of conceptual artists, our production designers, and the producers—Andrew talked about seeing Father Christmas not as a jolly old St. Nick with a bag of video games,

but as a wise old Norse warrior, returning home after years of battle, full of both hard-earned wisdom and love for the children.

One of our illustrators, Alan Lee, famous for his conceptual work on *The Lord of the Rings,* had been drawing while everyone else was talking. The sketch he produced was Andrew's vision on paper: the hearty old returning warrior, years of battles and generosity on his face, wearing the garments of an old Norse fighter rather than the familiar red and white of a shopping mall Santa Claus.

"Exactly," Andrew said, pleased with a great start on a fresh concept of the character.

And that's how it went for almost two years, page by page, character by character, creature by creature, castle by castle. Before we even began shooting, Andrew had literally put together the entire movie, shot by shot, on conceptual story-boards edited together with voicework and music.

13

OPPOSITE AND ABOVE: *Conceptual illustrations of Father Christmas.*

PREPRODUCTION

THE PRODUCTION TEAM

THERE ARE ONLY A FEW PEOPLE IN THE world capable of producing a movie this big. My first call to a producer was to Mark Johnson. I'd met Mark when I was a student at the University of Virginia, and he was an alumnus of the institution. Not only was he the most impressive person I'd ever met professionally in the film industry (among other credits, he'd won a Best Picture Oscar® for *Rain Man*); he also took time to be nice to a kid like me. So I kept in touch with him for years. When Walden Media's Cary Granat asked me to develop a list of potential producers, I convinced him that Mark should be at the top.

I called Mark up and asked him to read the book. I told him we wanted to make a faithful adaptation, I told him about Andrew, and we set up a meeting between the two.

Mark called me immediately after their meeting. In his modest fashion he said, "I'm not sure I'm who you want, but, boy, do you have the right director for this picture." Mark loved Andrew's vision for making a big-screen adaptation of his childhood imagination of the book. You need to know this about Mark: despite the Oscar®, despite the blockbusters, his favorite movie that he's produced was a small, wonderful kids' movie, *A Little Princess*. It was evident we had the right producer, too.

Cary says of our producer, "Mark did a fantastic job. As always he was a calm, steady partner to Andrew and the rest of the crew. He was a smart, creative, and experienced producer who was genuinely there every day."

With Mark in place we could build the rest of the team. No film of this magnitude goes off without hitting a few bumps. Since Phil Steuer has been working on movies since he was a boy, this veteran producer won't be rattled by anything. Truly unflappable, he is a problem solver unlike anyone else: A blizzard on the last day of shooting? "We'll figure it out." The steadicam's stuck in the mud? "I'll tell you what we're going to do . . ." Can't bring the reindeer into the country because of a Q-fever quarantine? "We'll build our own." We're running a little behind today? "We'll reschedule some things." Hurricane? Typhoon? Tornado? "No problem."

Cary Granat puts it perfectly: "As producer, he really stepped up. Cool, calm, very internal, funny, every day he was under attack from one area or another. Very little ruffled him. Just thinking about the move from North Island to South Island gives all of us an incredible appreciation for the job Phil did."

He also had an amazing production team. "What a troika," Cary says. "Production manager Beth DePatie has been our glue from the start. New Zealand production manager Tim Coddington was an awesome local hire. Very knowledgeable, talented, and a great problem solver." Tim was our right hand in New Zealand. And then there's "Slab," otherwise known as Rich Chapla, our production supervisor—the funniest guy on the shoot.

Most of the time you could find Slab overseeing the production of our film municipality at the foot of Flock Hill. Whether he was making sure the helicopters were up and running on time or finding a replacement for our special green screen tent that blew away in the gale-force winds of New Zealand spring, he kept the movie on track, no matter what curveballs were thrown his way.

Producers Mark Johnson and Philip Steuer make deals on the set.

LOCATION SCOUTS

We took a page from C. S. Lewis, who adopted mythology from all over the world into *The Chronicles of Narnia*, and explored the entire world for the best locations. Our extensive location scouts took us on snow hikes in the Czech Republic and Poland. We looked at Ireland, England, Canada, Australia, Argentina, even Antarctica. We left no stone unexplored.

In the Czech Republic and Poland, Andrew found the impressive natural stone bridge that the children cross in Narnia. They also found the perfect spot for Mr. Tumnus tucked away in a magnificent alcove among the rocks. Andrew found frozen forests there unlike anywhere else in the world—as if the White Witch herself had arrived and transformed it overnight with an alpine frost, wonderful, huge frozen lakes, and rock formations like nowhere else on the planet.

ABOVE: *Andrew's daily helicopter commute to the top of Flock Hill.*

RIGHT: *This is Earth? The magnificent otherworldly rock formations of Flock Hill.*

NEXT PAGES: *Stone Bridge location in the Czech Republic.*

Andrew brought the crew down to New Zealand for an extensive scout. He practically scouted the entire country, first by helicopter, then by foot, searching for the perfect locations.

He also started a few rumors. One day in the spring months before we began shooting, we noticed a news bulletin of special interest come across the AP wire. The report said we'd cast Nicole Kidman in the role of the White Witch. (In fact, to this day we've still never talked to Kidman or any of her handlers.) Apparently, someone who knew Kidman was taking a helicopter tour of New Zealand saw Andrew Adamson climb on board a helicopter and had mistaken him for the actress. From behind they are both tall with long blond hair.

"Andrew's a good-looking guy," says producer Mark Johnson, "but he's no Nicole Kidman."

We also owe a special debt of gratitude to our location manager, James Crowley, for making sure our production could get to these breathtaking spots. Whether he was clearing a boulder from the road to our camp or marking a trail up the mountain so the cast and crew wouldn't get lost among the immense rock formations, he was a constant force behind the scenes making sure we could shoot.

WRITING THE SCRIPT

We first brought in writer Ann Peacock for her gift of elegant simplicity. Ann worked hard with Andrew on drafting the immense initial outlines and structuring the earliest drafts. She lives in the middle of a giant redwood forest, an appropriate environment to inspire the fantastic world of Narnia. She was crucial in launching us on our way and rooted the wonderful, enchanting tone of the book to the screenplay.

The process of adaptation can be grueling. A scene can work well in a book but be difficult to imagine on-screen. Likewise, there are some things a movie requires that may not be in the original text. One of the rare occasions we veer slightly from the letter of the page is when Tumnus turns up in the White Witch's castle.

Andrew and Mark Johnson came up with the idea that since Tumnus is to be the emotional touchstone of the movie, it would be nice to see him again, at least once, before he disappears until the end of the movie. Andrew and the writers ran with this idea and crafted a poignant scene where Edmund meets a devout and bedraggled Tumnus in the White Witch's dungeon.

When it came time to enter the next phase of preproduction, we brought in screenwriters Christopher Markus and Stephen McFeely, a young writing team who'd impressed Andrew with a script they'd written about the life and death of Peter Sellers. They also impressed Andrew by how much they wanted the job. They took the script to the next level, focusing largely on character, bringing the children from the page to life on the giant movie screen.

We were very fortunate also to have access to Doug Gresham as our guide during the writing process. Andrew and the writers relied on Doug as a valuable resource. Sometimes if Andrew was deep in the middle of bringing a character to life or envisioning a scene, he would ask Doug what Jack (as C. S. Lewis was commonly known) was thinking when he originally conceived the idea in the book.

Revision after revision, until it was absolutely perfect, we finally had our shooting draft.

ABOVE: *Tumnus captured by the White Witch.*

RIGHT: *Conceptual illustration of Edmund sitting in the dungeon of the White Witch.*

THE PREVISUALIZATION PROCESS:
PRE-VIZ ANIMATICS

Working with a director who has an animation background had unforeseen benefits. Andrew employed the previsualization process in *Shrek* and *Shrek 2* to great effect. It was to be a new approach for those of us versed in live-action filmmaking. Now I can't imagine how anyone makes a film without it.

"Previsualization (or pre-viz) is a part of the filmmaking process whereby the director can visualize the movie through computer-generated cut scenes or animatics," explains previsualization supervisor Rpin Suwannath. "Where this technology used to lie within visual effects, its application has evolved into more of a story tool and pre-viz has become its own entity working closely with the art, camera, editorial, and visual effects departments.

"Essentially, a small group of artists under the guidance of the director can create the staging, pacing, and necessary timing for the film's specific scenes. Months before the cameras roll the director can achieve a clear vision of what they will need to build and shoot to tell the story."

ABOVE: *Pre-viz supervisor Rpin Suwannath.*

BELOW AND OPPOSITE: *A sampling of shots from the pre-viz animatics.*

Andrew and Rpin and the pre-viz artists spent the greater part of preproduction choreographing the massive final battle sequences years before the cameras even started rolling. The value was immeasurable: Andrew knew exactly what he wanted shot by shot before we even arrived in New Zealand.

"In addition, because the animatic files are based on real-world dimensions and lenses, the math behind the pictures can be applied to construction drawings and camera setups," Rpin points out, "as well as help producers break down the budget.

"At its core, however, pre-viz is about bringing all the elements of the script together in their most basic form to create a discussion point and eventual guide on how the film will come together in its final form."

Andrew reviewed the previsualization animatics every day with Rpin. No detail was too small, from the Phoenix's trajectory to the feasibility of a Gryphon's wingspan in relation to its ability to fly; they choreographed every sequence.

There's so much else involved in the preproduction process. Some of the most talented artists in the world spent years envisioning the world of Narnia, running around the world doing extensive visits with real-life beavers, lions, and foxes, workshopping location photos, doing historical research about London during the Blitz, cutting the animatics for the movie, staffing up with the best crew in the business, and conducting endless snow tests until Andrew found the perfect substitute for the real thing.

And this was every day for almost two years before we shot a single frame of film! Of course, all work and no play makes Narnia a dull place, so we did manage to fit in a little Ping-Pong and Foosball in that office, too.

CASTING

How on earth were we going to find four kids who were the right age, had the right character, were great actors, and looked like siblings to play the Pevensie children? This is one of the things I'm most proud of about this movie, because I think we really did something great with the kids we found.

In looking for the Pevensie children, Andrew was adamant about finding *real* kids—not Hollywood kids, not precious child actors, but *the real characters themselves.* Since in *The Lion, the Witch and the Wardrobe* all the action is filtered through the eyes of the children, they *had* to be real.

The first thing we did was bring in our children's casting director, Pippa Hall, who specialized in finding real kids in the United Kingdom. We'd worked with Pippa on a movie we made at Walden Media called *I Am David,* which starred a ten-year-old English boy who was an amazing actor; and we knew what outstanding work she'd done casting Jamie Bell in *Billy Elliot.* Jamie wasn't an acting student; he was a normal kid that Pippa found in one of the schools. We wanted to take this approach in casting *The Lion, the Witch and the Wardrobe.*

Thus began over two years of Pippa's going into schools and interviewing children for the four parts. She would go to a different school every day and interview the children. Then Andrew, Pippa, and I would watch each of the

Dear Pippa,   21st April 1999

Thank you for speaking to the Agents about me. I have met Julia Dickinson and she has taken me on. I have had some great fun in London. I hope my auditions go well but I haven't heard yet about one here last week. Thank you

from William (m)

PS I will phone to let you know what happens soon.

tapes—thousands of them—and we would choose who we thought might be worth bringing back.

Pippa had originally found William Moseley during a search for another movie four years earlier, and although he didn't get that part, she was impressed enough to write his headmistress a letter to single him out as an exceptional talent. He in turn wrote her a sincere thank-you note. When Pippa read our script, she immediately thought of William. He was perfect for the part of Peter—a pure, truehearted boy—and we loved him from the start. It was a similar situation with Anna Popplewell. She was on one of the earliest

Casting director Pippa Hall.

tapes, and she was a front-runner from the first time we saw her.

Six months later Pippa found Georgie Henley out of the blue when she went to visit a school in Yorkshire. We got an urgent call from Pippa after that casting session. She was bursting at the seams, said she'd found Lucy, and when we saw the tape we agreed: she was bright, articulate, and passionate, showing such a broad range of emotions in that first interview.

Skandar Keynes came to us last. We'd already narrowed down the other three finalists, but we weren't sure about our top Edmund choice. We had already looked at thousands of kids and done extensive London casting trips to workshop the finalists and were getting nervous that we still didn't have a favorite Edmund. So Pippa kept looking. And when she sent us a tape of Skandar, it was striking how much he resembled Georgie in both spirit and looks.

Pippa had met him a few weeks earlier when she was casting for another movie, *Nanny McPhee,* during a break from her work with us. Pippa loved him for Edmund and was terrified he'd get the part in the other movie. Fortunately for us, another boy got that part and Pippa was free to go after him.

But we almost didn't get Skandar after all. When we were doing the callbacks, his parents were on a trip to Tokyo, and his mother had forbidden him to go on auditions while they were away because his grandfather was looking after the kids and he had his hands full.

Pippa begged the head of Skandar's school to let him come in anyway. It all boiled down to Skandar. Did he really want the part?

So Skandar, knowing he wasn't allowed to do it, somehow coaxed his granddad into taking him to the audition anyway. We brought him in for a read-through of the whole script with Anna, William, and Georgie. Skandar nailed it.

We were so impressed with Skandar that we brought him back again the very next day to do one-on-one scenes with Andrew. We asked him to prepare only one scene, but it went so well that Andrew had him do others—and he didn't need pages. He'd memorized all his other scenes from the read-through!

His mother returned from Tokyo to discover we'd called her son back for the third day in a row. She seemed stunned. "You want to do *what* with my son?! You want him to star in your movie? In New Zealand?!"

These four kids—William, Anna, Georgie, and Skandar— weren't only wonderful individually; they were great *together.* "There was never a moment when I didn't really feel that they were all brothers and sisters," says Walden Media's Cary Granat. "They pulled off enormous emotion and humor and were just great kids to be around." We knew we had the right kids when it became clear they were a family.

FINDING THE CAST

By Pippa Hall, Children's Casting Director

ON GEORGIE HENLEY: I remember taking the train up to North Yorkshire to see Georgie's school. I'd already had to postpone the trip twice, and then I'd had to take a big train to a smaller train and transfer.

When I finally got to Georgie's drama group, I kept thinking, I just want to leave and catch the 5:30 train home. But then I saw Georgie, and she was so worth it. I stayed so long and was so excited by her—excited that we'd found our Lucy—that I almost missed the last train home!

ON SKANDAR KEYNES: Skandar was a little like a deer in the headlights at first; he was bemused. He had no idea what was going on. He thought he was coming back for a normal callback after the general workshop, but in fact

we were really interested in him for Edmund, and that night we sent him the top-secret script. He went to school that morning, showed up in his uniform, and came in for a read-through with three kids who obviously knew each other. He sat slightly away from the table and wondered what was going on the whole time. He had this look on his face the whole time like he'd just smelled something bad. But he was brilliant in the read-through. We kept looking at each other each time he'd read a line because he was so good. Then we called him back the next day—again!

ON ANNA POPPLEWELL: I met Anna early on. I had so many Susans to see. But Anna was so safe; she was just right. We kept looking anyway, but we never thought for a minute she couldn't do it. She kept coming back and we realized how perfect she was for this family. Not just a brilliant actress, but so consistent and stabilizing for the other kids. Great fun to have around, too. And she's so dedicated. During one of her breaks from school, Anna got the train out to the country to prepare with William. This was toward the end of the casting process, and they didn't even have the parts yet. It was well before the read-through and her screen test. She's so giving to everyone around her.

ON WILLIAM MOSELEY: When I got the script and read it for the first time, I immediately thought of William for the part of Peter. I hadn't seen him for years, but I went to see him again and I thought he was just perfect. Exactly the same, only four years older. Andrew was worried that he was too young and boyish, but we knew he had time for a growth spurt.

William had something we liked, but we had him work with some coaches. Near the end of the casting process, he was practicing scenes at home.

He would yell at cows in the field at home, "Soldiers of Aslan!" He would be standing in the middle of a field shouting at the cows. He built up his confidence level and *became* Peter.

ON THE PROCESS: We taped about two thousand kids. I screened at least four thousand. I'd go to local plays, loads of plays, schools everywhere. I'd sometimes go to a school and they'd throw hundreds of kids at me. I also got inundated from America. I had some families offer to fly their kids over just to meet with me for five minutes—all because they were such fans of the book.

The high point for me was the screen test. The casting process had gone on for so long. Finally I felt like the movie was really going to happen. The kids were such good fun that day, too. They were playing poker and snooker! I went around everywhere with a tape. Now I'm just dying to see the movie.

ON ANDREW ADAMSON: I remember thinking, when I first met Andrew, he's very cool; he's going to be nice to work with. He's very open. He was willing to say, "I've never done anything like this before. How do we do it?" And he's so patient. Normally directors watch the tapes for only a couple hours. Not a couple years.

William Moseley

Andrew's being so open made the kids more receptive. It helped a lot with the parents, too. A movie like this could have been so disruptive to family life. The parents really had to trust the crew. I think Andrew and Perry talked them into it, promised we'd take care of their kids.

27

WILLIAM MOSELEY

PETER PEVENSIE

WILLIAM *IS* PETER. WE GOT HIM AT JUST the right time in his life. On this movie he leapt from boy to man. "As corny as it sounds," he says, "I think that's the reason we were cast for these parts: we're so much like them."

A lot of us noticed that he shares Peter's strength of character. Doug Gresham recognized it the first time he saw William in a casting tape.

He called it "a strength of character." "We put William through hell for this part," producer Mark Johnson recalls. Enduring endless callbacks, workshops, and sessions with coaches before getting the part, William not only persevered but rose to the top.

In the four years since children's casting director Pippa Hall met William Moseley in auditioning kids for another movie, he had auditioned for many parts but never gotten one. He'd earn his way to the end as a finalist, but another boy would always end up getting the part.

All that rejection seems to have been a positive thing for William. Or at least *he turned it into something positive*, and that's part

OPPOSITE: *"Long live King Peter."*

LEFT: *William Moseley as Peter Pevensie.*

RIGHT: *Period costume drawings of Peter.*

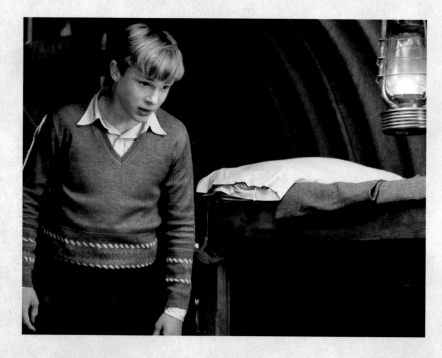

LEFT: *Will nails Peter's first big dramatic scene.*

OPPOSITE: *The Pevensie family recovers in their makeshift bomb shelter.*

of the magic of Will's character. The rejection kept him so grounded that even now there isn't any cockiness in him.

There were times when Will, like Peter in the book, would worry about his ability to see his family through, to make the scene work. He's incredibly conscientious. Whenever you see Peter trying hard to save his family and fix the world around him in the movie, you would also see Will trying to do the same thing in real life. It's what makes him shine as Peter.

This quality in Will, always striving to give his best, was evident on one of our first days of shooting. We began with a very dramatic scene: Peter hurries Edmund out of their house during the Blitz and they dive into the bomb shelter built in the backyard. Then they're in the bunker, having narrowly escaped the bombs.

That day William, normally gregarious and in the thick of things, sequestered himself in a remote corner of the soundstage to review his lines. You could see how hard he was working from the expression on his face, but there were just too many distractions.

Andrew, assessing the situation, took William to the train compartment at the far end of the set for a private word. From outside the detailed replica train, I saw the two of them really *talk*— very intimate, very private. Soon after they came out it was time for the cameras to roll. Everyone waited with bated breath: our first big dramatic scene, and it had to be great, it had to be powerful. Will took some deep breaths and waited for the cue. "Action!"

Will came out of the blocks on fire. He raced into the bunker, pushed Edmund to the ground, and gave an amazing speech about responsibility, about how Edmund could have gotten them all killed, about keeping the family safe. Everyone was speechless. One of the most powerful scenes in the movie, and Will nailed it on the first take.

And then Will looked down at his hands and saw that he was still clenching the door handle. He'd slammed the bunker door so hard behind him that he'd yanked the handle off. He was so involved in the scene that no one noticed until it was over.

The soundstage erupted in laughter. Welcome relief. Will's father, Peter Moseley, once said to me, "I don't think I've ever seen him truly unhappy." I think he's right. William has an

ability to appreciate life, to see the good in all things, and that appreciation is infectious. We saw that trait during his first callback, when we put together a workshop of some of our favorites to see where we stood. We put Will in a group with a potential Susan, Edmund, and Lucy and asked them to play a scene written especially for the audition: the Pevensie children play Ping-Pong to get Lucy's mind off being evacuated to the country. It was like pulling teeth to make the scene come alive, because most of the little girls

who came in for Lucy could barely read lines from a script. Andrew wisely asked the kids to improvise the scene, and he gave Will the simple goal of making his little sister in the audition forget her troubles, making her laugh.

Will was the only boy on the tapes of that workshop who made the little Lucy in his callback really *laugh*. Others went through the motions, and the little girls gave a few requisite giggles, but Will got his Lucy to have a good time. He got down on her level and talked to her,

On the Frozen River.

not as an actor in an audition, but as himself. He jumped around like a big goofball, unafraid of what anyone else would think, and made it his mission to make that little girl have a good time. He helped her smack the Ping-Pong ball around; he played with one hand tied behind his back; he hopped around and played on one foot; he juggled the ball on top of his head; and I think he even took the paddle in his teeth and hit the ball with it. Eventually the little girl at the audition was in hysterics.

He's a great big brother in real life, too, and this was an energy he brought to the role. With both a younger brother and sister, he knows a thing or two about looking after siblings. Not surprisingly, then, he developed a special bond with each of his movie siblings.

William and Anna befriended each other

immediately. We threw them together in a series of callback workshops, and they hit it off from the start. We ended up pairing them off to rehearse some scenes in an adjacent room, and Anna has told me since that they found a stack of head shots and rifled through everything they could get their hands on for any information to see whether they were going to get the parts. Those two held each other up throughout the movie. William showed up on set the very last day of shooting to support Anna even though he wasn't in the scene, and Anna invited Will to stay with her in London for the first costume fittings after we'd told them they had the parts.

Georgie took to him like a little sister almost before we got around to introducing them. She gave him grief about his oversized vintage belt buckle. (One thing you may not know about William is that he's a consummate thrift store shopper.) She made him laugh and the two immediately felt comfortable around each other. He looked out for her in the callbacks and screen test before they even got the parts, and she still gravitates toward him, looks to him to look out for her.

Then there's Skandar. Thank God we found William, who could appreciate Skandar's—let's call it his own special brand of spirited hijinks. Someone else might have thrown Skandar in the trash can, but from day one William loved Skandar's sense of humor. And Skandar loved having a partner in crime, a big brother to perform for.

Those two cut up every day on set. One day they were shooting a scene set in the Pevensie house where a bomb from the Blitz blows out their window. They loved the stunts in that scene: Will got to run in and throw Skandar to the ground, giving Skandar his first on-set bruise. Skandar had been giving Will such grief that, when they got up, Will told him that the soft, shattered stunt glass on the floor was made from sugar. Will knew that Skandar, who can be perfectly active without the help of any sweeteners, was banned from sugar on set— no candy, no chocolate, no soda. The next thing we knew Skandar was stuffing as much fake glass into his mouth as he could. Will doubled over with laughter as Skandar's face turned green at the awful taste.

They were so good at pushing each other's buttons that it was easy to forget they weren't real brothers. One day I gave them both a ride home after go-cart racing on our day off, the two horsing around in the backseat. When I pulled up to William's place and he got out of the car, I turned around and looked at Skandar.

"Well?" I said. Was he waiting for a written invitation to get out of the car?

"I don't live here," Skandar said, laughing at me.

ABOVE: *I love this shot Anna took of William giving Georgie a little cuddle in between takes. If you look to the right, you can see our first AD K. C. poking his head around the corner to come drag them off to set.*

BELOW: *Best friends. William hugs Anna on the Frozen River set after a long day of shooting.*

And leave it to William; he actually pulled out sentiment and emotion from Skandar, who so loathed touchy-feely warmth that his worst nightmare was the group hug. During the highly emotional battle scene where Peter sees that Edmund has been mortally wounded, Skandar noticed how genuinely upset William was. The emotions and pain were evident on his face, so much so that Skandar actually got up after the scene and gave his on-screen big brother a hug. "It was amazing," William remembers. "He hates hugs more than anything in the world!"

One day in the studio they discovered a room full of throwaway Styrofoam parts. For anyone who wants to find a place to play on a movie set, this is a dream. William and Skandar dove in and had a blast pulverizing the giant mound of harmless Styrofoam bits. Georgie had followed them into the room but didn't dive in like the boys. She stood off to the side, a little shy about joining in. Will noticed her and managed to get Skandar to stop tearing everything apart for a minute. They grabbed a

OPPOSITE: *Director Andrew Adamson prepares William for his fight with Maugrim the Wolf.*

ABOVE: *Regrouping after Peter kills the Wolf.*

nice, pliable sheet of Styrofoam and walked over to Georgie.

"Would you like to break one, too?" William asked Georgie in his perfect big-brother voice.

Georgie lit up. And one high karate kick later she split the board in two.

"It's funny," Will told me toward the end of our long shoot in New Zealand. "I was thinking today we're like a *real family*"—and they were.

It was also stunning to watch Will's transformation into a young man over the course of the movie. Andrew shot the movie in chronological order to allow the children to evolve as they do in the story. The idea was for the art to imitate life, but it was remarkable to watch the changes happen in front of our eyes. "When Peter steps through the wardrobe, he's a boy," William explains. "When he steps back out of the wardrobe, he's a man."

PREVIOUS PAGES, ABOVE, AND RIGHT: *Peter battles the White Witch.*

BELOW: *The Pevensies tend to Edmund on the battlefield.*

Once we were shooting the battle scenes on the South Island in New Zealand, months into the shoot, gone was the small, uncertain boy who'd been so worried about getting the scene right. Now William was suited up in full body armor and brandishing his sword riding bareback, dispatching Minotaurs, fighting for the forces of Aslan. Now it seemed effortless for him. One reason for this was Will's dedication to training. Allan Poppleton, our weapons instructor, physical trainer, and stunt coordinator, oversaw Will's transformation personally. On William's days off, it was common to find him either kickboxing at Allan's gym or sword training with him in the mess tent. On the rare occasion that he did have some free time, he always managed to fill it with physical activity that would help build him up for the upcoming battle. Whether it was our editorial department's weekly 8:00 A.M. Saturday basketball game, soccer during set breaks, or a tennis match first thing in the morning (I saw him use a great backhand with his broadsword that sent a Minotaur flying during one of the battle scenes), Will was determined to live up to our expectations. When his real-life brother came for a long visit, William found an opportunity to beef up his training and spend time with his little brother at the same time. They went to the hotel pool to swim laps, with William's little brother holding onto Will's legs for a better workout and for a free tow through the water.

Some of Andrew's most spectacular shots required William to ride bareback in full battle armor on Peter's steed. Most people who've never even tried to ride bareback would shrink at the challenge of riding at a full gallop with no harness or saddle or anything to keep you on the horse. Will's another story.

Even though he'd never done it before, he learned to ride bareback almost immediately, no small feat. We watched the first horseback riding dailies in amazement, often unable to tell the difference between William riding bareback and our expert stunt rider doing the same. His posture was perfect and the horse was galloping at full speed. Will was a natural.

From day one our animal trainer, Sled Reynolds, had to keep telling Will to slow down. He began riding bareback at a full gallop. But that's Will. He's as determined as Peter. He's the kind of person who will never slow down. He lives life at full throttle, and I don't think he'll ever stop.

By the time we filmed the battle sequences, William's hard work had paid off. He knew that by the time he reached the coronation at Cair Paravel, he had to become, according to the text, "a tall, deep chested man and a great warrior, and he was called King Peter the Magnificent."

On-screen and in life, William lives up to the title.

OPPOSITE: *Peter leads the charge into battle.*

LEFT AND RIGHT: *Peter's sword.*

ANNA POPPLEWELL

SUSAN PEVENSIE

ANNA WILL BE RUNNING THE COUNTRY one day. That's the kind of person she is: kind, compassionate, organized, extraordinarily talented, and just plain brilliant.

During a typical day, it was perfectly normal for us to find Anna rehearsing a scene, going to a costume fitting, posing for a photo shoot, finishing up a Latin essay on Pliny, and still having time to bake a cake for someone's birthday, finish a collage of pictures to send home to her friends, or share the latest cut of her documentary on the making of the movie. You could pop into Anna's trailer between scenes under the auspices of checking in on her, making sure she's doing okay, and moments later, she'd have you sitting down with a warm cup of tea discussing how *you* are doing.

I remember a night in Prague, when we came back late from shooting and dinner afterward, and there was only one person left in the hotel lounge, stretched out on the couch. It was Anna doing her school work. Anna tries to live every minute of every day to the absolute fullest.

There's both a graceful elegance and an innocence to Anna. It's rare to find both qualities in one person, but they reside together beautifully

LEFT: *Susan comforts Lucy.*

RIGHT: *Costume sketches of Susan.*

OPPOSITE: *Anna with her favorite props strung over her shoulder.*

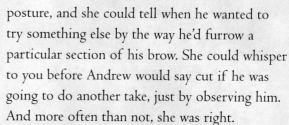

in Anna. "She's wise beyond her years," says producer Mark Johnson, "but she's still a girl."

Anna possesses a timeless, classic beauty that comes from the inside out. When she smiles, *your* whole face lights up with *her.*

"With Anna," continues Mark, "I feel like I'm talking to a peer. Her ability to catch the nuances of adults is extraordinary."

That's part of what makes her such a great actress. Her impersonations are priceless, there isn't an accent she can't do (though we tried to stump her), and she's a keen observer of people and life. As sharp as they come, perceptive to a fault, she certainly knew everything that happened on set, and everything underneath it all, too. She could tell when Andrew was pleased with a take by his posture, and she could tell when he wanted to try something else by the way he'd furrow a particular section of his brow. She could whisper to you before Andrew would say cut if he was going to do another take, just by observing him. And more often than not, she was right.

Anna is also utterly dependable. Even when we couldn't depend on the weather to cooperate, on the animals to hit their marks, or on the planes to be on schedule, we could always rely on Anna. "Anna is the acting Rock of Gibraltar," Mark says. "She never falters. Always there on the spot. Right on it."

One day we had a sudden change of plans and decided to shoot Skandar walking through the wardrobe into Narnia for the first time. The only problem was he'd already gone home for the day. Anna to the rescue. Since all we had to see were Skandar's feet and legs as he walked through coats and ended up in snow, Anna volunteered to put on his costume and do the part herself.

The Lion, the Witch and the Wardrobe was a movie she'd wanted to do for a long time. "I first heard about this part," Anna remembers, "over two years before I was cast. I was very excited about it, but you try never to get your hopes up, because often auditions just don't work out. If you're not right, you're not right."

As with William, the audition process was a long one. "I hardly remember the first audition actually, though I remember there were a few

---

TOP: *The first time with all four Pevensie children together, at the read-through.*

LEFT: *What a trouper. We needed to get some more shots of Skandar walking through the wardrobe into Narnia for the first time, but Skandar had already gone home for the day. So guess who filled in for him. Good thing we were only shooting it from the waist down.*

OPPOSITE: *Everyone but Skandar knows you sit on top of the chair.*

workshops that went quite well," Anna states in typically modest fashion. "The read-through was the first time we were all together. It went well and started to feel really good then." But even after all that time she wouldn't allow herself to think the part was hers. "Even at the screen test, I still didn't think I had it."

Well, the screen test certainly clinched it. In the script for that day, the scene where the Pevensies play hide-and-seek in the Professor's house began with an intentionally boring game: Susan was to read a word from the dictionary and ask her siblings to guess the word's origin.

According to our script, the word Susan was to pick was *gastrovascular*. We'd been doing that scene in callbacks for what seemed like years and it was starting to feel a little stale, so Andrew directed the kids to improvise for the screen test.

This time, the scene was to begin with Lucy picking any word from the dictionary, and Susan would take the scene from there. As the cameras

rolled, Georgie turned the page and shouted out a word that bears no repeating in this book—a word that an eight-year-old wouldn't know—but everyone else sure did.

There was a collective gasp on the soundstage, and I was sure we'd have to stop the scene and start over. We hadn't counted on Anna, who casually flipped the page, pointed to another word, and without missing a beat suggested to Georgie, "Let's try this word instead." And on she went with the scene, as if nothing had happened. True grace under pressure.

Of course, like most truly gifted actresses, Anna gives all the credit to the director. "I connected with Andrew," Anna says. "I just really liked him, liked talking with him." One of the things she values most about her director is that he gives his actors the perfect environment in which to flourish. "It's a laid-back set, and everyone's very friendly. Andrew is so relaxed that it makes everyone else relaxed."

Anna's innate understanding of the role under Andrew's direction really brought the character of Susan to life. "I can relate to Susan," Anna says about her character. "She thinks in terms of practicality. There are certain areas where we're very similar and certain areas where we're not. I feel very defensive of her. If anyone accuses Susan of being an outright cynic, I'll say, 'No, she's not. There's a perfectly logical explanation for it all. Don't talk about her like that!'"

Anna helps to bring out the best in others. "I think sometimes the work off camera that you don't get to see is some of the most important," Anna says. "If we're doing a scene and I have to get angry, then William will be off-screen when I'm doing my close-up and he'll try to make me angrier. He'll go out of his way to help me out. We all do the same for each other."

From the beginning Georgie looked to Anna for guidance on set. In an early scene where the Pevensie children have to spend their first night in the strange Professor's house, the scene requires Lucy to be sad and to give the line, "The sheets feel scratchy." It's an intimate moment, a tender confession for a little girl, and Georgie looked to Anna off-screen for support. Georgie, feeling a little tentative, searched over the bright lights and called out a timid, "Anna?" A comforting voice answered, "It's okay, Georgie; you can do it." And Georgie did.

Anna describes William as "very charismatic and very open—very good-looking, too. I've never had a big brother in real life, and now William has become one for me."

The first thing she noticed about Skandar were his eyes. "Skandar has these eyes that are really expressive and quite penetrating." Even more surprising, she remembers, "he was quite shy at first actually, believe it or not." Boy, did that change. "The first weeks on set he played loads of jokes."

Anna endeared herself to her adult costars, too. When Tilda Swinton, who plays the White Witch, heard that Anna, because of scheduling issues, was going to have to make the long trek from New Zealand to London all by herself, she volunteered to change her ticket so she could take Anna home herself. "She's awesome," Anna says about Tilda. "As in 'I am in awe of her,' but the moment you start talking to her, you realize she's friendly and very kind and down to earth."

OPPOSITE: *Anna brings out the best in others.*

ABOVE: *Anna and Will embrace on the last day of shooting in New Zealand.*

There were, however, some costars that she didn't like working with at all. And no, I'm not talking about Skandar. It was the mice, of all things—the ones that chewed through Aslan's bonds at the Stone Table. Andrew happened to ask her early on what things in life she was scared of. When she said mice, he laughed.

"I asked him what was so funny," she remembers. "And he said, 'You do realize you have a scene with mice.' At the time I just thought, oh, whatever. Since we have three

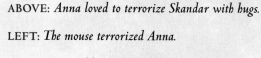

ABOVE: *Anna loved to terrorize Skandar with hugs.*

LEFT: *The mouse terrorized Anna.*

OPPOSITE: *Tilda with Anna and Georgie.*

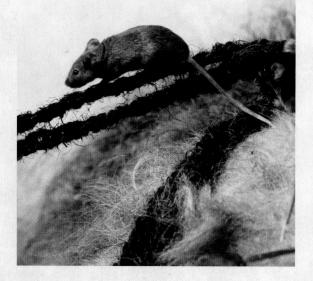

billion animated creatures in this film, why would the mice be real?"

When it came time to work on the scene, Andrew said to her, "You know they're real mice, don't you?" But, Anna recalls, "He's so good at playing jokes on people, I didn't know he was serious. Then the day before we filmed the scene, he called me onto the set and said, 'Good morning, this is Mr. Jingles.' He had a mouse in his hand, and I freaked out. I squealed and cried and felt sick. Andrew could finally see I wasn't

kidding, so he arranged for my double, Ashley, to do the parts with the actual mice. None of the stuff you see with the mice is actually me."

Incidentally, Georgie loved Mr. Jingles. She was so fond of him, in fact, that Andrew told Georgie she could bring Mr. Jingles home for a night. Georgie's mom, Helen, quickly vetoed that idea.

Anna will miss lots of things about working with Andrew. "He's so good at maintaining a balance between work and play," she says. "And he knows exactly what's going on in your head; he's so good at reading people. I'll miss just knowing that he's there to talk to."

"There's a scene when we got to the Beavers' house and Mr. Beaver is cracking jokes and Andrew was trying to make us laugh. He was playing Mr. Beaver and at the time it was just so funny. We'd been doing all these scenes where we'd been running away or we'd been scared or

distraught over Edmund, or thinking this is awful and we have to go home. Suddenly we're doing this scene where we were all laughing and we had such fun filming it. Andrew was doing impressions of us and the crew members. It was hilarious."

One favorite sequence of hers was the coronation scene at Cair Paravel. "I loved it," Anna says, "because it came at a point where we were leaving Auckland after four months of filming there, and everyone got to dress up in really nice clothes and they looked great and the set was gorgeous. It was a really nice moment because everyone was happy and having fun."

OPPOSITE: *Beaver Dam.*

BOTTOM: *Andrew and friends.*

NEXT PAGES: *The Pevensies as guests of the Beavers.*

The dress she got to wear for the coronation scene was her favorite costume. "It's so pretty." This compliment means a lot from a girl who really knows how to dress. Anna dressed up as her fashion icon, Holly Golightly from *Breakfast at Tiffany's*, for Howard Berger's and KNB's Halloween party. Don't get me started on her shopping talents.

all the people who have been through those experiences in real life."

As conscientious as Anna was about getting the scene right, Andrew was equally committed. "He was fantastic at giving us direction," Anna remembers. "He talked to me and Georgie about sad things and made us really put ourselves in our characters' shoes at that point. He got us to

"And my least favorite was probably Susan's schoolgirl shirt and skirt. I completely understand why Susan would wear it. It's just not very Anna."

The most challenging scene for Anna came when Susan and Lucy had to witness Aslan's fate at the Stone Table. "Watching Aslan die was my favorite scene to shoot—and also the worst because it was so hard," Anna says. "It was difficult because even though I've lost grandparents, I haven't been in front of someone dying, and if you haven't really been there it's something you can't easily imagine. You feel as though if you don't do it right, you're insulting

watch some of the filming of the actual scene at the Stone Table. It was pretty intense. We spent two days solid crying."

Although the Stone Table was her favorite scene from an acting standpoint, her real pride and joy were Susan's bow and arrows, which she learned to wield with great precision. There's a great shot in the movie where Aslan and all the resurrected statues from the White Witch's courtyard are at the edge of a cliff with Susan and Lucy, overlooking the battle raging below.

OPPOSITE: *Susan the Gentle.*

ABOVE: *The prophecy fulfilled.*

The White Witch and her troops look up to see that Aslan and the reinforcements have arrived to turn the tide of the battle. Leading the charge, next to Aslan, is Susan, her bow and arrow poised high in the air. The scene ends there.

But when we were shooting, Anna, deep into the moment, surprised everyone by letting one of her arrows fly. She smiled demurely. "Sorry," she said. "I just had to do that." So now, somewhere in the depths of the valley below Flock Hill on the South Island of New Zealand, Susan's lone arrow remains, waiting to be found by an adventurous, keen-sighted fan.

She turned sixteen on set during the climactic battle sequence and celebrated her sweet sixteenth in an army tent with hundreds of extras suited up in prosthetics, and tons of creatures. Boggles and Ogres and Minotaurs and Satyrs and Centaurs and Dwarfs and Dryads all came together to celebrate Anna's sixteenth birthday!

She made friends with everyone, cast and crew, creatures and designers. They all rallied around Anna. At the wrap party, Anna was the only one who got up in front of our army of crew and extras and thanked Andrew and everyone for such a wonderful production. Graceful and articulate to the very end.

She'll miss each and every one of them when she returns home. "I will definitely see all the Pevensies when we get back," she vows. "I live around the corner from Skandar, so I'm not going to be able to escape."

There's no doubt in my mind that the transition back to normal life will be easy for Anna. She's as real as they come. She was ready to get back into the normal swing of things, ready to get back to her studies, her activities, her friends and family, ready to get back to real life. Toward the end of filming she said wistfully, "It's gone more quickly than I expected; the time has really flown past. It's a bit like a long and lovely dream," she explains, "and now I'm ready to wake up."

On the Flock Hill set, Anna lets one of her arrows fly.

59

SKANDAR KEYNES

EDMUND PEVENSIE

WE ACTUALLY THOUGHT HE WAS GOING to be the quiet one. It seems crazy now, but in those first auditions, it was evident to all of us that Skandar didn't have nearly as much to say as the other kids we cast.

Boy, were we wrong. Skandar turned out to be the life of the production. We could always tell when he was on set, not just because we could hear him but because he had an infectious energy that rubbed off on everyone. His spirit spread through the entire production the minute he walked on set, as if someone had finally turned on the lights.

He even had his own catchphrase— "Hi, everybody!"—every time he entered a room. It was a wake-up call to enjoy the movie, enjoy this crazy adventure, share in the fun with Skandar.

It doesn't hurt that he's a brilliant actor. Not that he'd admit it. Playing Edmund, according to Skandar, was a natural fit. "Well, let's see," he says, "Edmund is the black sheep of the family, the outcast. He's always trying to get

OPPOSITE: *Edmund tries out the White Witch's throne.*

LEFT: *Playing hide-and-seek in the Professor's house.*

RIGHT: *Costume sketches of Edmund.*

up to the level of the older two by putting down Lucy. He's very immature and full of resentment.

"Now when Edmund changes in the story and starts to get good," he adds, "*that* part was hard."

"As much as he's part of the family," says producer Mark Johnson, "he's always a little bit on the outside. He's a perfect Edmund, one of a kind."

Despite the natural fit, Skandar was utterly serious about his work. And yet he never took himself too seriously. He was as willing to laugh at himself as he was at anyone else.

There's a great scene at the end of the movie when the four Pevensie children come tumbling back out of the wardrobe and find the Professor waiting for them. Jim Broadbent, who plays the Professor, tosses a cricket ball at the kids for one of them to catch. In one take, he gave it a little too much oomph and it whizzed by and smacked Skandar right in the face.

Everyone stopped in that pregnant moment where you're not sure if you should laugh or attend to the wounded. We waited for Skandar's reaction. In just a second he burst out laughing as hard as he could, after which everyone else laughed, too.

There's something very telling about that story. Everyone laughed because Skandar did. That's the way he is. When you're around him, laughter is contagious. He has tremendous spirit, almost impossibly contained in a thirteen-year-old body.

Oddly enough, we didn't find Skandar until very late in the audition process, but in no time whatsoever, he became the front-runner for the part. After a general callback with hundreds of

Jim Broadbent is about to bean Skandar in the head with a cricket ball.

kids, we called him back the very next day for a read-through of the entire script. "I was given the whole script, and it was massive," he remembers. "I thought, Okay this is great, but I hope they don't expect me to learn all of this overnight!"

We loved what he did in the read-through, so we asked him back. "I thought I was coming in for just one audition," Skandar says. "But I ended up coming in Monday, then Wednesday for the read-through, and then Friday to work on scenes with Andrew."

The read-through was intimidating for Skandar because he'd had the script for only twenty-four hours and there he was acting it out with kids who'd been doing the scenes for a long time by then. "They all seemed like they'd known each other for a long time, and I was really nervous about the audition. We'd be reading through a scene and suddenly Will would be

looking right at me and not reading the script, and I kept thinking, How does everyone else know these scenes by heart? I kept looking up at everyone as I read the script, trying to keep eye contact, so I'd look like I knew what I was doing."

The tapes of that first read-through show that Skandar was genuinely uncomfortable with these new "siblings." But it was only partly nerves. When he was shooting pool with William before the read-through, he leaned over for a hard shot and his pants split completely through the rear. During the entire read-through, he was trying to make sure his pants stayed together.

Two days later, when Andrew called Skandar back to workshop with him alone, he asked the young actor to work through a scene that he hadn't been told to prepare for. "Hold on," Andrew said. "We'll get you the pages."

"No, that's okay," Skandar said. "I know it." And he did. The whole script.

"That's because I had a very bad experience once," Skandar recalls. "I went back ten times and was the front-runner for a part, but I didn't get it in the end. They'd sent the whole script and I'd learned only the one scene they'd told me to prepare. But when I got to the last audition they told me they expected me to know all my scenes by heart. So from then on, every audition I go to I learn all my lines."

Of course, Skandar wasn't *all* dedication. Once the movie got rolling, it didn't take long for the youngster's less serious side to make itself known. He'd sneak up behind producer Phil Steuer and poke him at the beginning of every day on set. We'd see Phil—possibly the most relaxed person on the planet—jump a mile up

LEFT: *During rehearsals the kids discovered Skandar hated the group hug.*

OPPOSITE: *Philip Steuer strongarms Skandar.*

out of his seat, and that's how we'd know the day had started.

Likewise, we knew it was time to shoot a scene when first assistant director K. C. Hodenfield would shout, "Skan-DAR!" A common thundering cry on set, it was the signal that it was time to quit horsing around and start shooting.

Normally, that cry was followed by an immediate plea of innocence from Skandar: "I didn't do anything!" But the camera doesn't lie. When Anna was shooting her making-of-the-movie documentary, she captured a shot of Skandar, Will, and Georgie working in front of another camera. When that camera stopped rolling, Skandar put his hands around Georgie's neck, pretending that he was about to strangle his little sister. Georgie shouted out, in her best K. C. voice, "Skan-DAR!" He stuck his hands in his pocket and proclaimed his innocence: "It wasn't me; I didn't do anything!" But Anna got the whole thing on tape. When she screened her doc for all of us, that scene got the biggest laugh. Even from Skandar. Busted.

Eventually, it was time for payback.

Skandar's favorite joke from the movie isn't one he played on someone. It was a joke played on him.

"It was the coronation bit, at Cair Paravel," Skandar recalls. "Will had a scene where he danced with a Dryad, and Anna had a scene where she danced with the Fox. It wasn't in the script for me to do any dancing, and Andrew thought maybe I'd feel left out and suddenly said, 'You're dancing.' I thought he was joking at first, and then he said, 'No, you're really dancing.' Will and Anna and everyone else in the scene had been rehearsing their steps for a long time, and I started to panic because I hadn't learned anything. But Andrew said don't worry, we'll teach you tomorrow. So the next day I arrived on set, ready to dance, and there was this woman and

it was strange because a lot of her moves were very . . . adult, if you get what I mean. Some gyrating, some pelvic thrusts!

"I kept thinking this can't be right, can it? And after we'd rehearsed it a few times, they kept asking me if I was ready for them to roll the camera, and I kept telling them I wasn't because I was so freaked out by the whole thing. Then

ABOVE: *Andrew Adamson prepares Skandar for battle.*

BELOW: *Skandar being fitted for armor.*

OPPOSITE: *Edmund ready to strike.*

out of the corner of my eye I thought I saw Andrew and K. C. snickering with the rest of the crew. I figured out it was a big joke when she asked me to do the chest bumps. The whole set cracked up and laughed."

"He has a wonderful darkness while being really sensitive and smart," observes Andrew. You can look at Skandar's face and see the morality tale of the story playing out, see the inner struggle. He's that good.

The scene Skandar found most difficult to film was "the emotional scene, the crying bit, when Tilda turns the Fox to stone and I give away information. But Andrew helped me loads. Before we shot the scene he pulled me aside and talked to me about some personal things which I won't repeat." Whatever they talked about worked: the scene is *powerful*.

"He's magical," Skandar says about his director. "He's great with children. Amazingly fun and cool and funny. Lots of hair, too."

Andrew was the only person on the set who could render Skandar speechless. Every time he had something funny to say about Skandar, the kid who had a comeback for everything couldn't find the right words.

"It's true; it's so annoying," Skandar says. "I can counter everyone but Andrew. One day, because he's always taking the mick out of me, I'm going to have the best comeback ever. I'm going to call him up thirty years from now and say, 'Hey Andrew, remember when you said this? Well . . . '"

Skandar enjoyed taking part in the battle scenes. He trained hard to learn proper sword fighting. "I loved it," Skandar says. "Our sword trainer, Allan Poppleton, is always making jokes about how my weak spot is if people tickle me in the stomach. So we'd be learning the facts of the sword fight and he would tell me what moves to do and then he'd tell Tilda, "Just hit him like this," and then he'd poke me in the stomach and start tickling me and I'd lose it."

The training must have paid off, because Edmund's valiant performance in battle with the White Witch remains one of the movie's highlights.

The horse racing was fun for Skandar, too, but it didn't always go smoothly. "Will and I were riding our horses one day, and in one take my horse, Phillip, developed an attitude problem. Will's horse was standing still, and Phillip decided to go straight for him. I was trying to turn him desperately, and he just went bang into the other horse."

The trouble didn't end there. "He's not just a vicious horse; he's also very competitive. One time Will and I were monkeying about in the middle of a take, just cantering around, and Will decided to go into a gallop. I didn't even touch Phillip, but suddenly he was galloping to the top, trying to beat the other horse and going way too fast. I thought he was going to run off the cliff." Skandar finally managed to get him to calm down, "but that was the last time we could ride him."

Skandar, who enjoys playing cricket at home, didn't like filming the cricket scene in the movie because he had to pretend he was bad. "For safety reasons during rehearsal we had to use a rubber ball, which had a really strange bounce that made it hard to hit. Then when we were finally using the real ball for the scene, Will bowled it wide of me every single time so I couldn't hit it. I was furious. Then Andrew started to doubt that I could actually play cricket, and he asked me to *pretend* to hit the ball for the rest of the rehearsals. On the next ball, I hit it as hard as I could. It smashed into some of our lighting, and the crew yelled, 'Skan-DAR!'"

You wouldn't necessarily assume that a cut-up like Skandar is also a brilliant student, but he is. Especially in math; the kid aces everything. (We're considering letting him do a pass of the budget for the sequel to see if there's anything we missed.)

While shooting the battle scenes, Skandar would have to sit down on top of the mountain for lessons during his breaks. I asked one of his teachers how he was doing one day, and she said he was remarkable. "After five hours of standing on a rock and doing the same thing a hundred times over, he still sat down and did the lesson," she said. "He was completely into it, did really well and completed quite a lot of work in a short span of time. He even managed to feign enthusiasm."

He doesn't have to feign enthusiasm for his costars.

He says he'll miss having William around: "When it's all over I won't miss the bruises he gave me to impress girls, or the occasional scar which will give me a story to tell my grandchildren, but I'll definitely miss the pranks and the laughing and all the making fun of each other. I'll miss all the funky advice he gives me about everything—football, girls, video games, clothes. Most of all, I'll miss having an older brother."

About Anna, he says, "She's so smart. And we're both fans of Arsenal (their soccer team at

RIGHT: *Skandar's last time riding the horse.*

NEXT PAGES: *Skandar and Will racing.*

Edmund meets the White Witch.

home), so she has good taste."

"When I first met Georgie," Skandar says with a laugh, "she was very eager to talk." But seriously, he adds, "Georgie is great. She's small and she's hilarious. To laugh at. I mean *with*—to laugh *with*." You can tell he had no problem playing the annoying brother.

Of all the kids, Skandar has the most scenes with the White Witch. I asked him what it was like to meet Tilda Swinton for the first time. Though he didn't know it initially, we kept her contact with him limited to give the first time they met on-screen a genuine element of surprise. (We did the same thing with Lucy and Tumnus, to great effect.)

"I remember meeting her and she was very professional. We were doing rehearsals together at first, but at the end of each one she'd disappear. Then after our first filmed scene Andrew said to Tilda, 'You can go ahead and talk to him.' Then she said, 'Hey, we can talk now.' And I said, 'I *thought* something was weird.'

"The next day we went for lunch, and then that weekend we saw *Zoolander* together. And after that every time I saw her I said, 'Hey, Matilde,' which is this line from the movie, and then we'd do the poses ('Blue Steel!'). And then if we ever pretended to have an argument, 'It's a walk-off!'" (Another line from the movie.)

"Another time she took us all out to play miniature golf. Tilda laughed because on the first shot I whacked the ball into a sign that said, 'This is not a driving range.'"

Although Skandar grew a great deal during the movie, both in height—six inches and

counting—and in maturity, he's still firmly in touch with his inner child. His favorite things to do are "playing football with my best friend, Theo, and of course video games—that's the heart and soul of my life." He'd rather play video games than eat or sleep. Though he's grown up in some wonderful ways, he still talks a mile a minute, the same Skandar who never let our spirits lag.

Near the end of the movie, Pippa Hall asked Skandar's ever-patient mother, Zelfa, what her favorite day of shooting had been. Zelfa replied that it was the scene in the White Witch's camp, where Skandar was tied to a tree, bound and gagged, perfectly silent. "Can we reshoot that one?" she asked.

Is your seat comfortable, sir?

He was pretty quiet at the wrap party, too, when Andrew took him aside (as he did all the kids) for a private moment. "I'm very proud of you," Andrew said. "Uh, yeah, okay, sure," Skandar replied. He took another sip of his Coke and patted Andrew on the shoulder. "I'm proud of you, too."

Skandar understands the enormity of what he's been involved in, knows the special place this magical movie will occupy in his life. "It's crazy," he says. "It's amazing. It's a once-in-a-lifetime experience."

And that's exactly how it is to work with Skandar: a once-in-a-lifetime experience.

GEORGIE HENLEY

LUCY PEVENSIE

TRANSLATING THIS BOOK INTO A MOVIE would never have worked without Georgie Henley. Someone had to make Lucy Pevensie real. That was perhaps our greatest task: finding the little girl whose imagination and faith in things hard to believe in would launch us into the world of Narnia. She had to be unique—wise beyond her years, but innocent as the purest child.

The fictional Lucy is special, and we had to find someone just as special in real life. Fans wouldn't settle for anything less. That's an awfully big responsibility for one little girl.

It's fitting that Georgie is the one who leads us into Narnia for the first time. She has the most wonderful imagination of anyone I've ever met. I bet she could even give C. S. Lewis himself a run for his money. She could inspire anyone to go through the wardrobe.

We got an excited call from Pippa one night over a year before we began shooting. "Listen, I have someone very special to show you," she said. "I'm really excited about her."

The tape excited us, too. Georgie handled Pippa's questions beautifully. Sometimes Pippa would break the ice by asking a question: "If you were starving on a desert island with the rest of your

LEFT: *In the Professor's house.*

RIGHT: *Costume sketches of Lucy.*

OPPOSITE: *Lucy discovers Narnia.*

Professor Kirke comforts Lucy.

family and there was nothing left to eat, who would you eat first?"

Before Pippa could finish asking it, Georgie blurted out, "My sister!" With a devilish grin, she then proceeded to describe exactly how she would go about gobbling her up, head to stinky toe. In other words, she got the joke and ran with it. A good sign that she could handle all the adults and long hours and hard work that come with a movie.

But she could handle the sad end of the spectrum, too. When Pippa asked her what she was reading at the moment, Georgie described the plight of the young heroine of a novel titled *Bed and Breakfast Star*, her eyes carrying the weight of the protagonist's struggles. Georgie's eyes darted outside the window and she whispered, "It's a bit sad."

Andrew was blown away by Georgie's tape, by her remarkable range. He knew at that very moment—after seeing *thousands* of children in over a year of auditions—who his Lucy Pevensie would be. He pinned Georgie's picture at the top of his wall of finalist photos, and the family began to take shape from there.

"She seemed really curious," explains producer Mark Johnson. "Like the kind of little girl who would really go into the wardrobe."

Of course, it was still a long time before Georgie officially got the part. There were auditions, callbacks, read-throughs, a screen test. And there was the small matter of convincing her parents to trust us with their daughter, who'd never professionally acted in anything, halfway around the world for the greater part of a year.

Of her first meeting with Andrew, Georgie says, "I thought he was a girl at first. I was far away from him and he's so fair; his hair and skin looked quite light. Then I got close and saw the beard and thought, Oh it's just a guy with long hair."

Despite that initial confusion, it didn't take long for them to hit their stride. Creatively they were communicating from the outset on a telepathic level. During the first round of callbacks Georgie was acting in a scene that Andrew had created for the movie—a scene that we'd spent the greater part of a week in London watching hundreds of kids work through. As the children discuss whether to stay behind to fight for Narnia or return to the safety of their own world, Edmund finally owns up to his own grave mistakes and urges the family to stay behind to right his wrongs. While this particular Edmund was pouring his heart out emotionally, Georgie reached over and grabbed the little boy's hand for support.

We were stunned. We weren't used to seeing an eight-year-old improvise, but she added the one perfect, supportive, caring gesture the scene needed. Of *course* that's what Lucy would do: she loves her brother; she's always there for him.

Andrew looked up from the camera and gave each of us a look. He was in awe. This was Lucy.

Her imagination was always at work when we were shooting, too. It's one of the reasons she's so good in the film. "I sometimes had to talk her out of scenes," Andrew recalls, "because she can scare herself. She imagines real wolves chasing her, and she's really in the moment."

Even though she's a great actress, she's still a little girl. There was the time we gave all the kids iPods as a start gift. We'd downloaded all seven of the Narnia Chronicles from books-on-tape so that they'd have something to do during their downtime on set. When Georgie opened hers she simply exclaimed, "Thank you *so* much!" After we left, once we were safely out of earshot, she leaned over to her mother, Helen, and whispered, "What is it?"

The movie itself wasn't enough to satisfy all Georgie's creative impulses, and so she kept a mini tape-recorder on hand to conduct periodic interviews with cast and crew and to record her own thoughts as she embarked on this great adventure. Her colored pencils and sketch paper were never far away either. She also managed to write two books in her spare time. The first, *The Snow Stag,* is in the author's words "a story about a mythical stag who has mythical powers. This guy called Mark is trying to protect it, and this guy called Roger is trying to kill it." Next is *A Pillar of Secrets,* which Georgie describes as the story of "an emerald green pillar in Antarctica, and then a girl named Tanya, who lives in England. She's got very green eyes—emerald in fact."

Georgie loves school. Most young actors might find juggling their acting responsibilities with schoolwork to be quite a challange. Not Georgie. "One time I came back into school from the set," she remembers, "and I told the teacher, 'Mum said I'm allowed to stay another hour if you ring her straightaway when I'm finished.'" But her mother had said no such thing; she was sitting in the car waiting. "She wasn't happy when she found out," Georgie admits, "but it was worth it."

When she thinks about what she wants to be when she grows up, the possibilities are many. "Actress," she told me. "No, don't make it an actress; I want to be an author. No, don't make it an author; I want to be a professional cartoonist."

Georgie has no trouble relating to Lucy's finer qualities, pointing out the girls' similarities: "She's

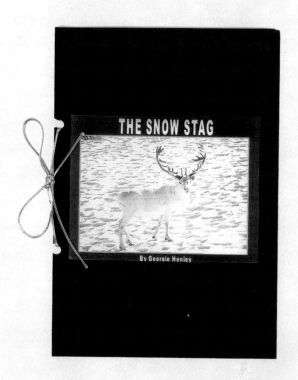

ABOVE: *Georgie's* The Snow Stag.

BELOW: *Georgie's* A Pillar of Secrets.

quite forgiving and she always likes to laugh. Also, she's quite outgoing." There are differences, too: "I think I'm a *bit* brave, but Lucy is *very* brave." Still, that didn't stop her from wanting a bigger sword to use in battle.

Georgie doesn't have to think long about what she'd love to take home from the set. "It would be my belt, with my dagger and my vial," she says—Lucy's gifts from Father Christmas. "And if I was allowed to bring three things home I'd also like a Dwarf's sword, because they fit me perfectly."

She says she and William "just clicked." She looks up to him like a brother, and he takes care of her as if she were a little sister.

And about Skandar? Well, he's not all *that* bad. "One time he was doing this scene where he had to be mean to me—the scene where Edmund betrays me about going to Narnia, where no one believes me. Afterward at lunch time he came up to me and gave me this great big hug."

Then she nails one of Skandar's greatest qualities—something she says she'll miss greatly

81

ABOVE: *Father Christmas gives Lucy the cordial.*

OPPOSITE: *Lucy's gifts.*

As the youngest in a family of three girls, Georgie knows a thing or two about playing a little sister. Thoughts of her on-screen big sister bring out the poet in Georgie. "Beautiful butterfly angel," she offers, when allowed just a few words. She adds, "Anna is always there when you need her."

when the movie is done: "He has a special ability to make people laugh."

No film version of *The Lion, the Witch and the Wardrobe* would be complete without the magical relationship between Lucy and Tumnus. What charges their scenes with so much emotion and depth is the magical friendship that Georgie and James McAvoy enjoy in real life.

She remembers the first time she met James. "Well, he came in and I was expecting to see a

blond guy with green eyes and a greasy look to him." And where did she get this impression? "I watched one episode of his TV series *Shameless*, and because of the character he plays I thought he was going to be this really uptight guy. I thought he'd have green eyes from the book so he could bore into you. I thought he'd have a bit of a greasy look to him."

But when she finally met James in person, all those false impressions vanished. "He had piercing blue eyes, lovely eyes, nice curly chestnut hair," she recalls. "And he was wearing this cool vintage jumper and trainers. Then he thanked someone for bringing him a salad and he turned to me and he said, 'So how're we doing?'"

They hit it off from the start. Georgie loved her scenes with James. Their chemistry is palpable; you can see two people who enjoyed hanging around each other, and it makes such a difference to the movie.

Rehearsals were fun, even when they had to work them around James's hectic TV schedule. He was on a plane back and forth from London to New Zealand with sometimes less than a day of turnaround time.

When they practiced the race through the forest where Tumnus decides to help Lucy escape, Georgie discovered just how much James was there for her. "We had to jump over a mattress," Georgie recalls, "and one time when I jumped I tripped and almost landed on my stomach. But before I hit the ground, James jumped out and caught me. He had his arms

ABOVE: *Georgie's drawing of Tumnus.*

OPPOSITE: *Lucy meets Tumnus.*

NEXT PAGES: *Lucy in Tumnus's house.*

wrapped around me and said, 'White knight in shining armor?' Then he said, 'Are you all right, darling?'"

"I apologized for being heavy," Georgie says, "and he said, 'Not as heavy as I expected.' I thought, Wow, this is a nice guy."

To heighten the element of surprise when Lucy first meets Tumnus, Andrew went to great lengths to make sure Georgie never saw James in full Faun makeup until it was time to shoot the scene. You'll see in the movie that Georgie's surprise at seeing Tumnus for the first time is one hundred percent real. That first meeting is pure magic.

"I screamed!" Georgie says. "I jumped behind the lamp-post and I went up to him and I said after, 'James! Look at you!'" She didn't mind doing the additional takes. "It was so fun screaming!" she says.

The first day of shooting didn't go as smoothly, at least not from Georgie's perspective. We did a scene where the children are sitting in the train car as they're evacuated to the countryside. Andrew talked them through the scene, and then we captured our first shot, then another, and another. The kids were fantastic, and they felt charged with a thrill of satisfaction and relief.

All of them but Georgie, who looked distraught even though she'd performed perfectly. A few takes later we discovered the problem. She hadn't realized it's typical to shoot the same scene several times from different angles in order to have

different takes to piece together in the edit room. This being Georgie's first movie, she thought we were reshooting because she'd messed up.

"I didn't know we would be doing them over and over again, that all day we'd be doing the same shot," Georgie remembers. "I cried and cried because I thought, 'I can't get it right!'" She laughs about it now, because she figured out that this is how things work on a film set.

Other parts of the movie were nothing but fun for her. She had a ball dressing up in all the different outfits. Among her favorites is the dress

ABOVE: *"The biggest and the littlest." Patrick Kake, who played Oreius the Centaur, had the biggest sword in the movie. Weta Workshop was very proud of that one. Georgie, by comparison as Lucy, had the smallest.*

OPPOSITE: *Lucy and Susan at target practice.*

NEXT PAGES: *Lucy and Susan react upon seeing Tumnus turned to stone by the White Witch.*

she wears when she meets Tumnus for the first time. "I love that one," she says. "My little cardigan." Other favorites include the regal dress she wears for the coronation scene.

"That's my favorite-ever costume, when I'm on the balcony with Tumnus." But she's quick to add, "Oh yeah, I have a third, which is my yellow nightie with pink roses and green roses and gum boots."

She found time to make friends and have fun on set, and that's important for a movie with kids. There are so many ways Georgie has grown over the course of the film. Physically, she's right behind Skandar as far as growth-spurts go. At last check she'd grown three inches. By the time they reach the coronation scene, you can see that Lucy the girl is showing signs of becoming Lucy the young woman. I think it choked up her mom to see Georgie in that Queen's dress for the first time.

And she's still the same little girl we fell in love with in that first audition. Some things will never change. The way she looks up to Will for comfort and fun, to Anna for guidance, and to Skandar because no matter how much they spar, she's nuts about him. She's the same little girl who said she'd gobble up her sister if she were starving on a desert island, the same little girl who danced her pants off with Anna to Christmas songs on the last day of shooting, the same little girl who cried real tears when she saw Aslan on the Stone Table.

When the filming was done, she went right back to school, seamlessly resuming her normal life. You could say she handled the transition so well because she's strong and resilient and well adjusted, and all of that's true; but there's something extra-special about Georgie that tells you she's always going to get the most out of life. It's the same quality that makes Lucy Pevensie so special; Georgie has an infinite sense of wonder. And we're lucky to have her share it with us in the movie.

At the end of the production, Georgie wrote Andrew a heartfelt thank-you letter. He was genuinely touched by what she had to say. She thanked him for trusting her and for taking her on this incredible journey, and then she added, "You understand the best in me." Andrew certainly did.

The truth is, when the movie comes out, everyone else will know the best in her, too.

TILDA SWINTON

JADIS, THE WHITE WITCH

THE MOST IMPORTANT THING TO REMEMBER about Tilda is that she's the exact opposite of the White Witch. The fact that she can pull off playing the ultimate paragon of evil shows what a stellar actress she is. She's first and foremost a mother, a lover of life, an artist and patron of the arts, an inspiration, a passionate friend, a woman of immense talent, and a generous soul.

The first time I met Tilda, I was struck by how perfect she would be for the movie. She was in New York to present an esteemed award to her fashion-designer friends Viktor & Rolf, who'd used her as their muse for their latest line.

I'd heard about her before that through her agent, Brian Swardstrom, who's a good friend of mine. Right after we won the rights to the Narnia Chronicles, Brian urged me to meet Tilda. I'd been blown away by her performances in *Orlando* and *The Deep End* and was excited to meet someone of such exceptional talent.

When we met for a scheduled lunch, she had a terrible cough. She took great pains to protect me from any germs. I could already see the mother in her, straining to take care of everyone around her.

Tilda is about six feet tall and has long, elegant limbs, perfect porcelain skin, fiery red hair, and eyes that could melt your heart or just melt you, depending on her intent. I've never met someone with as much *presence* as Tilda. When she walks into a room, you know you're in for something special. Those of you who

---

OPPOSITE: *Her Imperial Majesty Jadis.*

LEFT: *The White Witch prepares for battle.*

RIGHT: *Costume sketches of the White Witch.*

know the White Witch's origin from reading *The Magician's Nephew* will know what I mean when I say that I could believe she comes from the royal family of Charn.

We both talked a mile a minute about movies we loved, art and music we were passionate about, life in general. A consummate conversationalist, Tilda also practices the fine art of listening. She had plenty to ask about me and the project, and she listened attentively as I related our plans to make a faithful adaptation of the classic. I mentioned that though it was way too soon to think about cast, Brian had told me I had to consider her for the role of the White Witch.

When I'd finished, Tilda reached into her coat pocket and fished out a couple of snapshots. She handed me the pictures: her twins posing with her in her backyard at home in Scotland.

"You see, I'm perfect for this movie," she said, "because I *live* in Narnia."

I stared down at one picture—at the gorgeous rolling hills of green, the cliffs and mountains in the distance, the animated trees that seemed alive with human characteristics. Her beautiful children, Xavier and Honor, wore joyful expressions that were a little

mischievous, elfin, ethereal. I looked up from the photo to their mother and studied her otherworldly grace, an elegance that transcends anything else I've seen on this planet. She really *did* live in Narnia.

The casting process is always a long one. Andrew pored over movies and lists, considering legions of actresses as he searched for the woman who would bring to life the White Witch Jadis, her Imperial Majesty, that frigid tyrant who'd thrown Narnia into a hundred-year winter and callously dispatched all her enemies with the simple wave of her stone-turning wand.

When Tilda met with Andrew for the first time, he was very impressed with her take on a small role she'd just played in the movie *Constantine*. She'd played the role of the angel Gabriel. But unlike the conventional take on the character, Tilda explained, she played him as an avenging angel full of ruthless rage. In his mind, this was how he "saved" people.

Andrew liked what he heard. He took her on a tour of all our conceptual art: all the various creatures, all the magical settings, the White Witch's castle made of ice—Tilda loved what she saw.

When Andrew narrowed down his list of finalists for the part, I remember getting a call from Cary Granat late at night at home while I was packing to go to London for one of our many casting trips. He asked if I'd seen this red-haired English actress who played the judge in a little-seen but critically praised movie called *The Statement*.

"What's her name?" I asked and reached for my toothbrush.

"Tilda Swinton," he said.

As we refined the search, we met with casting directors in London, hoping to hire the perfect person for the casting job. Gail Stevens

LEFT: *Casting director Gail Stevens.*

CENTER: *Conceptual sketch for the White Witch's wand.*

OPPOSITE: *The White Witch on her throne.*

NEXT PAGES: *Conceptual painting for the White Witch's ice castle.*

came to the meeting with an inspired list of choices for each of the adult roles.

"Who are you thinking of for the White Witch?" Andrew asked.

"Tilda Swinton."

We hired Gail the next day. (A wise decision on our part: she introduced us to James McAvoy among others, thus finding us our Tumnus as well!)

We asked Tilda to fly down from Scotland to meet Andrew in person for dinner. She hopped on a plane at a moment's notice, joining us for sushi and a discussion of the part. She and Andrew shared the same vision, as it turned out. I remember that as Andrew explained more and more about his vision for the White Witch, the waiter dumped an entire platter of sashimi on Tilda's lap.

Tilda smiled and laughed. Nothing could wrinkle her. This was merely a baptism.

Though she understands Jadis's evil nature, Tilda is one of the most giving people I know. This is an incredibly valuable trait on the set of a challenging movie. Hollywood stars aren't typically known for their generosity and warmth. Tilda is an exception. I saw this firsthand when we were shooting in a forest on the coast of New Zealand's North Island, called Conifer Grove, working on scenes of the White Witch's makeshift camp. It was the first time that we'd been free of the soundstages and that we had our menagerie of prosthetic creatures and real-life wolves with us. It was freezing cold and it rained nonstop. On top of that, we had smoke and fog machines going.

Not a word of complaint from Tilda. Nothing but encouragement for those around her. She held court with a host of exotic creatures who couldn't see a thing through their prosthetic heads, and who could barely breathe. After each take, as soon as the camera stopped rolling, Tilda made the rounds, asking how people were holding up. Then, after some private words of encouragement, maybe a laugh or two, she'd return to her spot in time for the next take.

Tilda's home became a destination for everyone after work, a haven for people to get together and relax. On any given day after wrap, it was common to stop by Tilda's, where she'd light a bonfire in her yard and cast and crew would come together: Dwarfs and Centaurs and Minotaurs and prosthetics artists and weapons experts and costume dressers and stuntmen. Tilda would arrive home after an impossibly long day, light the fire, and crank up some David Bowie, and the party could get started.

OPPOSITE: *The White Witch at her camp.*

ABOVE: *A few members of the White Witch's army.*

NEXT PAGES: *The White Witch at Aslan's camp.*

It was a normal sight to walk by the mess tent and find Tilda there in the middle of a group of extras and crew, sometimes singing with a guitar-playing Ogre, sometimes reviewing a book of sketches an artistic Centaur had brought in to show her. She insisted on staying after wrap

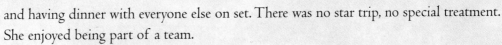

and having dinner with everyone else on set. There was no star trip, no special treatment. She enjoyed being part of a team.

One day on top of the mountain during an exceptionally crazy weather day, I remember seeing Tilda sitting on a giant rock while we shot a series of battle sequences. Sometimes other cast or stuntmen would sit with her, sometimes crew members. By the afternoon, when the torrential downpours started, I asked her if it was okay that we were making her wait so long for the shot.

"Oh I'm not shooting today; it's my day off," Tilda said. "I'm just here for support."

She took a particular interest in the kids. After a few days on set, she spoke to the producers about them. "We need to make sure the children are having *fun*," she urged. That was an assignment she took personally. One day she gathered up all the Pevensie children and their families and took them out for a lunch by the helipad and then out for a round of miniature golf down the street.

What matters most, perhaps, is that Tilda is one of the all-time greatest actresses. The first time I showed the C. S. Lewis Company the dailies of the sacrifice scene at the Stone Table, we were chilled by her performance. Her shriek when she

LEFT: *The White Witch emerges from Aslan's tent.*

BELOW: *The Pevensies react.*

NEXT PAGES: *The Stone Table.*

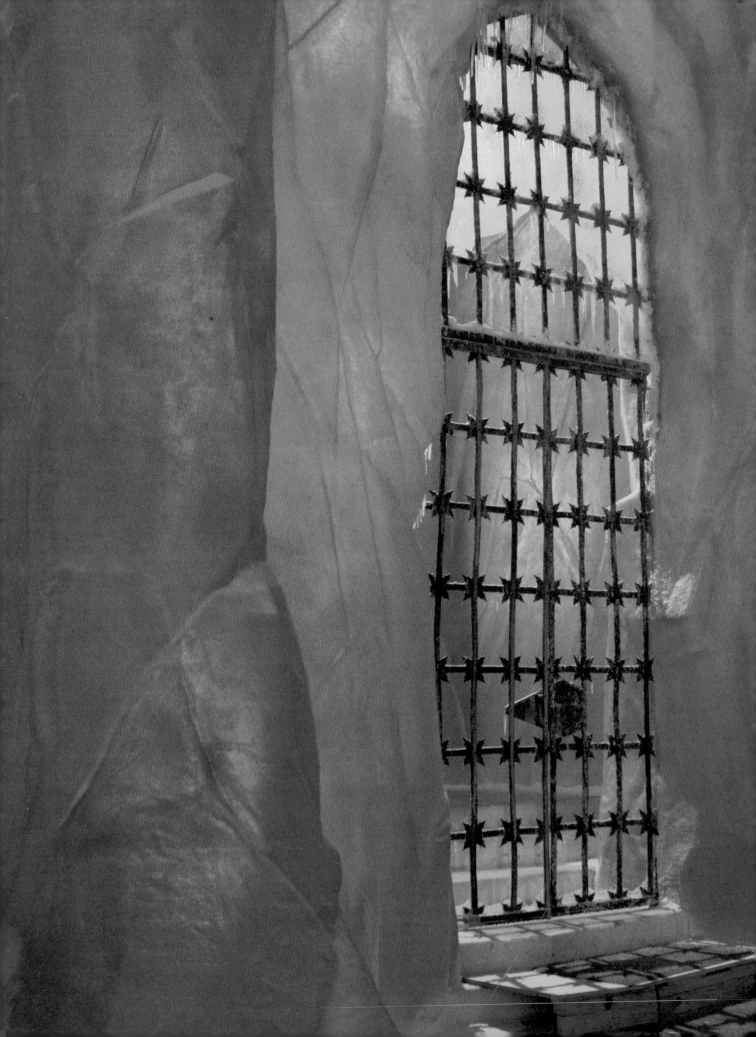

declares her enemy is dead will go down as one of the most bone-chilling sequences in film history.

Embarrassed at the emotion I felt on seeing the scene, I was relieved to note that Doug Gresham had tears in his eyes as well. "I'm sorry," he said, wiping his cheek. "I've just waited so long to see this story done, and now, to see it done right — it's what I always imagined."

Tilda can do more with a glance, a simple modulation of the lip, a subtle shift of her eyebrow than anyone else I've ever seen. We were constantly in awe of her talent and ability.

Her dedication to the training was immense. I remember walking into a tent one day where she was practicing sword training with our masterful trainer Allan Poppleton. She'd been learning to wield two swords at once for the first time. I saw a splotch of red on Allan's knuckle. "What happened to you?" I asked. "She got me," Allan said, gesturing to the wound. "I couldn't pull away in time." Guess she was getting the hang of it.

And she never complained, though the rigidity of her massive gown and the weight of her headdress, wig, and crown were enough to hobble an ordinary human. We rigged a board, known as her "board of pain," a stiff backboard with arm rests so that she could stand up and lean back in between takes and take the enormous weight off her neck. Over the course of a few days, the board became decorated with pictures of her children and friends.

Sometimes the costumes were so enormous that we had to put her in her very own White Witch–mobile to drive her to the set once she was dressed. In the beautifully designed and shot scene in the White Witch's dungeon, where she interrogates Edmund and Tumnus, Tilda discovered that her outfit wouldn't fit through the gate. A consummate pro, she wedged herself through and nailed the scene. Not only did she never complain; she made it seem *effortless*. The woman is grace personified.

She has a wicked sense of humor to boot, one that comes out right when it's most needed. With all the Weta Workshop teams working on the battle scenes those last two months of shooting, we saw a lot of commemorative T-shirts from *The Lord of the Rings*. Tilda had her own T-shirt made to wear on set: *LORD OF THE RINGS:* I WASN'T IN IT.

On the last day of shooting on top of the mountain, I boarded the helicopter with Tilda. We strapped ourselves in, and the pilot gave us the ride of a lifetime. As we dove down off the cliffs into the mist below, Tilda whooped and hollered and lifted her hands in the air with delight like she was riding a roller coaster. I was cowering in the backseat praying I wouldn't throw up, and she was having the time of her life. It's an image of Tilda I'll carry with me forever.

At the wrap party, Tilda told me this wasn't an occasion to be sad, even though our incredible adventure was coming to a close. It was more as if we'd been preparing all day for a wonderful dinner party, a special banquet, and now that we had all the ingredients it was time to prepare for the feast.

She inspired the best in all of us, and this movie wouldn't be the same without her. If life is truly a banquet, then surely Tilda will always sit at the head of the table, making sure everyone enjoys the feast.

ANNA'S JOURNAL: A NARNIA DIARY

Tuesday, June 22, 2004

I'm just on my way home from day one of shooting. It was *so much fun!* I can't wait to get up and do it all again tomorrow.

We were showered with gifts and attention this morning and I'm feeling rather spoiled. Perry bought us all beautiful journals and Parker pens. Philip Steuer gave us all stunningly bound lamppost miniscripts. I've even got moon boots and Uggs!

We shot the scene in the train carriage today. It was lovely to see sets and costumes and makeup all put together. Very 1940s! Everyone on set made me feel so welcome and special.

We also met all the teachers and saw the schoolroom. All nice but I think I'm looking forward to that part slightly less. Well, I know I'll sleep tonight at any rate.

Wednesday, June 23, 2004

Today we did some pretty intense scenes in the air-raid shelter. The crew had a flame torch for an explosion effect. K. C. said to Georgie, "Don't worry, our lifeguard is a trained professional." She replied, "Yeah, soon to be a trained professional with burned hands."

Georgie and I were crying during Will and Skandar's performance. They and Judy, who plays our mother, were totally awesome.

I've begun reading *To Kill a Mockingbird* and Will and I are reading it together—a bit of a joke! Everyone keeps saying what a wonderful story it is, and Perry has lent me the DVD. We're going to do a movie night at Andrew's!

Thursday, June 24, 2004

Today we shot the scene where Lucy is upset by the radio and we try to comfort her. First lines, first close-up—fun stuff!

Skandar got the digital camera and started taking all these photos right in Philip Steuer's face, saying, "Flashing! Flashing!" (which you have to say so the lighting crew doesn't think a lightbulb has exploded). Philip grabbed the camera off him and then simultaneously snapped him with the camera and wrestled him to the ground. We all saw a new, cheeky side of Philip.

It was strange today. Lots of people end up taking photos of you on set, whether for continuity or lighting or whatever. So I wasn't expecting anything extraordinary when someone asked me if he could photograph my profile and the back of my head. He then revealed the shots are for modeling our characters in the video game of the movie. I think it's completely bizarre!

After the radio scene we began the scene where Georgie slips out of bed to check if Narnia is real. I had to snore. Think I must have been fairly realistic since Georgie has now christened me "Miss Piggy Snorer!"

Today is the anniversary of my grandfather's death. Kay, our lovely driver, is taking us to throw some roses in the sea, because his ashes were scattered at sea.

Friday, June 25, 2004

End of week 1. It's been so much fun. Today we were filming the scene where Edmund betrays Lucy to Susan and Peter after they return from Narnia together. (We also finished off the snoring stuff.) I've been in pajamas all day!

Georgie had to cry in the last shot. She was fantastic! It's really nice to be working with so many people you feel you can trust.

Wednesday, June 30, 2004

Mum left this morning at 6:45 A.M. It was very hard saying good-bye to her and I'll really miss her. I'm surrounded by lovely, generous, incredible people, but they're not Mum!

We were finishing off the train station scene today and I was directed to appear vulnerable, insecure, and fighting back tears because I knew I'd miss my mum. Surreal how timing was so appropriate! Didn't require much acting.

The extras were lovely, and I'm rather sorry to see them go. A lovely girl called Lizzy gave us all presents and I was so touched I didn't know what to say.

I met Douglas Gresham today, very nice man. It's nice to know there are people looking out for C. S. Lewis's wishes.

Monday, July 5, 2004

Today we did the Mrs. Macready scene, arriving at the Professor's house. It was rather long and dragging actually. Not sure why. Still fun! I think I still find it hard to get used to the idea of spending a whole day on one scene.

Quote of the day: K. C., our first AD, said, "Skandar, you are a walking imposition!" Ha ha, that really made me laugh.

We are at the Henderson soundstage for the rest of the week now to shoot interiors. It will be nice not to have to move around!

K. C. gives everybody these tea tree–flavored toothpicks. Georgie was chewing one today, walking around like a mini–New York gangster.

Monday, July 12, 2004

We really had a lot of fun today. We were on location at Monte Cecilia House. The weather behaved perfectly. First we filmed all the cricket scenes. Skandar managed to get hit by the cricket ball several times.

Just after lunch, Helen Clark, the prime minister of New Zealand, came! She was lovely. I really liked her, and we did our first bit of press. Then later this afternoon, we did the shot where Mrs. Macready drives us up to the Professor's house in the horse-drawn buggy. Elizabeth Hawthorne, who plays Mrs. Macready, drove it really well.

Wednesday, July 14, 2004

We finished off yesterday's scenes. Then we went on to tumbling out of the wardrobe to return from Narnia. We started blocking the scene in the Professor's study.

The study set looks incredible, absolutely amazing. It's full of these great little knickknacks and neat little artifacts, etc.

Jim Broadbent is a legend. He looks great in his wig and beard and everything. It's so cool!

Tomorrow I have a late call. 11:00 A.M.! But that does mean it'll probably be a rather late wrap.

Mum had a newspaper reporter knocking on the door yesterday. Scary how quickly news travels.

Thursday, July 15, 2004

We shot about half of the scenes in the Professor's study, which I found slightly difficult to begin with. I think I had just talked about it too much and with too many people. I usually find it easier when I just do it. Anyway, I think we cracked it.

It was funny. They had to do this shot on second unit where a fly buzzes and buzzes until it dies and stops. The Humane Society doesn't allow a fly to die on camera. They had to use a frozen fly, which spun around buzzing as it defrosted!

Tuesday, July 20, 2004

We did a hide-and-seek scene where I have to hide in this old chest. It was so weird. The chest was over five hundred years old! Andrew kept joking around and saying it was an old coffin.

I met James McAvoy today, who is playing Mr. Tumnus. He's extremely nice. I love his Scottish accent!

Monday, July 26, 2004

Today was the first day I spent in Narnia. The Lantern Waste set at Kelly Park is completely incredible. It's huge and really stunning.

The snow is made out of finely dustified paper. The whole set has to be resnowed between takes. The dust really gets in your throat and eyes and nose. Everybody walks around in masks. Unfortunately, hospital masks aren't strictly 1940s and we can't wear them on set.

Oh, we got to wear our fur coats today. I love my coat! I also got to throw snowballs at Skandar. Ah yes, I have enjoyed my day.

Wednesday, July 28, 2004

Today we were filming the scene where we find Tumnus's door knocked off its hinges. We also shot the scene soon after it where we come out and meet Mr. Beaver for the first time. We had a stuffed animal/live model for Mr. Beaver. Half the time we were acting to that and the other half to a tennis ball on a long pole, with Andrew reading lines. It was really hard to resist the temptation to look up at Andrew instead of at the stuffed model!

We were all in our luscious coats again. It is so tempting to tread in the fresh paper snow. In fact, William and Skandar often succumb to temptation. Ha ha. Then the entire set has to be resnowed.

Monday, August 30, 2004

Today has been the first day of what's sure to be a trying and truly technical week. We're on the Frozen Waterfall with the ice blocks on hydraulics. They're really cool, water spurting and rocking, and there's fake snow all over the place. Every take requires about a forty-minute resetting. It's good fun, though. The scene's extremely intense and very dramatic. We're fully armed and bow-and-arrowed.

Tuesday, August 31, 2004

Today we continued with the endless Frozen River scene. We just went to a screening of some edited footage: the railway scene and also the Lucy-meets-Tumnus stuff. It looked really gorgeous: the photography is amazing. The meeting of Lucy and Mr. Tumnus was truly magical. Georgie, Skandar, and Will were all wonderful. I am of course overcritical of my own performance, but there you go. It does all look terrific.

Friday, September 17, 2004

Funniest of all funny things. Today Skandar had to go home quite early because he'd had an early call this morning, and they sent his double, Graham, home early as well. Anyway, they then had to do a shot of Skandar's feet as he falls out of the wardrobe, so guess who did Skandar's stunts? *Yours truly!* And I did it in one take. I can't wait to see Skandar's face tomorrow when I tell him.

Tuesday, September 21, 2004

I spent most of the day doing tunnel running with Georgie and William. I have to say that running through four-foot tunnels hunched over is not my fave, but I still had fun.

I've been doing my archery, which is improving and so cool. I'm now learning to do a quick, smooth draw so I can look really flash.

Friday, September 24, 2004

Today was very eventful. We did the scene where we reach the White Witch's courtyard and then Aslan breathes life into Tumnus.

Georgie looked very pretty in her dress, and I love my long hair extensions. It's almost as long as my hair was before they cut it at the beginning of the production.

Then at lunch time, Andrew showed all the cast and crew seven minutes of the film cut together. It's being shown as a trailer at a big marketing meeting at the Disneyland hotel. I have to say it really did look fab. Luckily, it didn't give me time to analyze and criticize my performance because it went by so fast. The photography was beautiful and the music really brought it to life.

Monday, October 4, 2004

We did the Aslan death scene—well, the scene after his death when Georgie and I are sobbing over him. It was really challenging, but very fulfilling. Georgie and I are all cried out.

I was cyber-scanned last week to enable the CGI guys to computer-generate me.

I've been fitted for my coronation party frock. It's absolutely gorgeous—crushed pale blue velvet with satin bucket sleeves. Awesome!

Tomorrow we're doing the scene where Aslan comes back to life. I'm really missing Skandar and William, as we haven't seen them for a few weeks. It's been just Georgie and me.

Andrew really makes me laugh by doing this hilarious accent. He always says "Yer bloiynd, yung man!" Ha ha ha ha.

Monday, October 11, 2004

On Friday I had an abundance of fittings and other preparation for the coronation. It's all very exciting. My dress and hairdo are gorgeous. My dancing is not. Picture the scene: Will and I prancing around the room, instructed to improvise a "mixture of formal medieval and Hungarian folk dance." Most amusing. Not that the choreography is bad; it's just that my partner, the Fox, is two feet tall and completely imaginary.

Wednesday, October 13, 2004

Today and yesterday we were at Muriwai Downs shooting the Narnia bathing scenes. Yesterday we kick-started with some cold paddling and splashing, which was followed today by a little tree climbing and more freezing splashing. Really, it was great fun, but we're only halfway through. The costume department has been truly fantastic, providing space blankets, puffer jackets, hot-water bottles, electric heaters, gloves, heat packs, thermals, wet suits, and all the rest of it.

Saturday, October 30, 2004

We've been "coronating" all week for the coronation scene at Cair Paravel. I've done lots of dancing with my imaginary foxy friend.

Tonight the prosthetics department is holding a mandatory dress-up Halloween party. Should be good. I'm going to be Miss Holly Golightly from *Breakfast at Tiffany's*. Mum is going to be a pussycat.

Wednesday, November 3, 2004

Yesterday we had our first day shooting on location at Elephant Rocks. I did my archery, which went really well. Georgie did her dagger throwing—pretty cool indeed.

The scenery here is beautiful. The mountains and the sea and the hills are awe inspiring and make you feel so tiny. It really is all it's cracked up to be and more!

Friday, November 12, 2004

We did the scene where the White Witch arrives at Aslan's camp. It was pretty incredible with so many creatures. General Otmin the Minotaur is seriously scary, and it's rather disconcerting when the animatronic Cyclops's eyes turn to glare at you!

There were lots of Fauns and Satyrs as well. There must have been over three hundred people on set!

GEORGIE'S INTERVIEWS: GOING BEHIND THE SCENES

Georgie conducted a series of interviews with her mini-recorder during the movie. Here are Georgie's interviews with some of her friends on the set.

INTERVIEW WITH ACTOR JAMES MCAVOY

GEORGIE: I'm here with the fabulous James McAvoy, who plays Tumnus. How do you like Auckland, where we're filming?

JAMES: It's a wonderful, very clean city, and it's been nice to visit the Sky Tower and stuff like that, which I know you've been up yourself. I'm enjoying it a lot.

GEORGIE: Do you like playing the role of Mr. Tumnus?

JAMES: I do like it. He's one of my favorite characters from all the books I read when I was a kid, but it's quite hard because you never thought it would be as hard as it really is. Like when you're doing it, you have to do all these weird things, sometimes get very sad, for instance, and I never really thought about that when I first got the part. So yeah, I do like it, but it's weird because there's stuff in it that I didn't expect.

GEORGIE: Do you think that you're like Tumnus in a way?

JAMES: No, I think Tumnus is more . . . he likes his toast and tea a little bit more than I do. And he likes his cozy fires a bit more than I do. If he had it his way, he'd probably never leave the house. He'd sit and read books the entire day long.

GEORGIE: So are you having lots of fun here?

JAMES: Oh yeah, it's been great! There's this really cool girl playing Lucy. She has energy the likes of which I've never seen in my life. It's as if the sun had exploded and all the energy had been put in her tiny little body.

GEORGIE: Auckland is a nice environment, with all the beaches and stuff. What in your opinion is the scenery like for you?

JAMES: I think it's very beautiful — it's very dark, you know, quite like Scotland, where I'm from, in a lot of ways.

GEORGIE: It can be a bit graphic sometimes.

JAMES: The black sand beaches and stuff, it's all quite gritty, quite scary, too, you know. It's beautiful, very beautiful, but it's very intense, I think.

GEORGIE: And at night it must get quite freaky because there's a lot of strange rocks on the beach, aren't there?

JAMES: I haven't been out there at night, have you?

GEORGIE: There's a lot of strange rocks and I haven't been out there at night, but at night I bet they would look very strange, wouldn't they?

JAMES: I would imagine so, but I get scared in my hotel room on my own at night sometimes. I'm not kidding. Sometimes I have to phone my girlfriend and ask her to just talk to me for ten minutes before I go to sleep. Which happened a little while ago because a scary movie, which I'm not going to tell you the name of, was on TV and I knew I shouldn't have watched it, but I watched fifteen minutes of it and then turned it off, and I couldn't sleep for four hours. I was lying awake in bed.

GEORGIE: But you're having fun, aren't you?

JAMES: Yeah, lots, oh yeah, that didn't ruin my fun. Not that one night. No, it's nice, it's all good.

GEORGIE: So you like it then?

JAMES: Everything's pretty darn fine apart from the fact that I've got a cold at the moment. So I've been taking fifteen vitamin tablets a day, but it doesn't seem to have done anything.

Georgie and James.

GEORGIE: So thank you very much, James.

JAMES: Thank you very much.

GEORGIE: That was very nice of you.

JAMES: I hope to come back sometime.

GEORGIE: Thank you.

JAMES: We're just shaking hands.

GEORGIE: This is Georgie Henley. Thank you very much, James.

INTERVIEW WITH MAKEUP ARTIST
NIKKI GOOLEY

Nikki Gooley making up Georgie.

GEORGIE: I'm here in the makeup bus with Nikki Gooley, a wonderful makeup artist. Nikki, how do you like working on *The Lion, the Witch and the Wardrobe*, working with the actors and the rest of the crew?

NIKKI: This is the best bunch of actors I've ever worked with. They're so professional. They let us do anything to them. We pull their hair and put hot rollers in—

GEORGIE: You're telling me!

NIKKI: And put horrible creams on their faces and we have a good time in here, don't we, Georgie? We listen to funky music.

GEORGIE: Which is off at the moment. What happened to the music?

NIKKI: For the copyright. In case you publish your story, we can't have music because of the copyright.

GEORGIE: Well, it was really nice talking to you, Nikki. Thank you very much.

NIKKI: You're welcome!

GEORGIE: Okay, this is me, Georgie, bye!

INTERVIEW WITH WETA CRAFTSMAN
JOE DUNCKLEY

GEORGIE: I'm here with Joe Dunckley, who's looking after us on set and organizes our weapons and props from Weta Workshop. He looks after William's sword and his shield, my dagger and scabbard and vial, and Anna's horn and her bow and arrows and quiver. A very talented man, and Weta a very talented group. So how do you like being in New Zealand, Joe?

JOE: Well, actually, I'm *from* New Zealand, Georgie. I'm from Dunedin, right down at the bottom of the South Island. I look after the props from Weta Workshop where they make them. I make sure everything looks the way they intended them to.

GEORGIE: How do you like working on *The Lion, the Witch and the Wardrobe*?

JOE: I love it. Everyone is really friendly, all the actors and crew. I'm really lucky in that a lot of my friends from childhood work for Weta Workshop as well. Rob is the other standby for Weta, and I've known him since I was five. We played soccer together when we were little. Now we work for the same company and we pretty much do the same job. I'm lucky like that!

GEORGIE: The weapons and the armor and all the things that Weta people design and make: How do you think the audience will respond to them?

JOE: I hope the audience will like them. The designers go to great lengths to make the props believable for the audience, but I think it's also for the actors themselves, so it's easier for them to get into character, believing the objects they're dealing with. That's important, too.

GEORGIE: You know that William has his sword and I have my dagger, and William really likes his sword. How did you know that he wouldn't just throw it out by accident and maybe cut down a tree or something?

JOE: Well, I suppose all you can do is explain to an actor the dangers, the risks, and then you just have to trust them with the props they've been given. Usually people don't understand that there are safety issues and concerns even if it doesn't seem like it's dangerous. Things need to be respected, and I think they are. It's going well.

GEORGIE: How do you think people will respond to this movie?

JOE: I think it's going to be really successful. The book has been around for a few generations, so you're going to have adults that have loved the book as children and they're going to want to bring their children as well.

Georgie and the sword she would rather have used in battle.

INTERVIEW WITH ACTRESS
ANNA POPPLEWELL

GEORGIE: I'm here with Anna Popplewell, who plays Susan. She's one of my best mates.

ANNA: And you are also one of my best mates, Georgie Henley.

GEORGIE: How do you like being in New Zealand and working on the movie, Anna?

ANNA: I'm really enjoying it. I'm missing everything at home, but it's really nice to be out here with such lovely people. It's like being on one giant holiday. It's great to be a part of something with so much magic — both in terms of actual magic in the film and also in terms of what's going on in this production.

GEORGIE: Ahem . . .

ANNA: Oh yeah, and Georgie Henley's all right as well.

GEORGIE: Do you relate to the character of Susan?

ANNA: Quite a lot. I certainly have some of her sense of logic, and I understand the idea of her trying to look after her younger siblings and growing up before she should really.

GEORGIE: How do you get on with the actors and with Andrew?

ANNA: It's really nice working with William and Skandar and you, because it's like having your best friends and your brothers and sister all in one. I've never been with a group of children where we're all different ages but we all get on so well. Georgie and I have been doing scenes without the boys for a couple of weeks now and we're really missing them.

GEORGIE: Which is very unlike us, I assure you.

ANNA: The cast I really get on with — Tilda Swinton is so lovely; it's great to work with Jim Broadbent, and James McAvoy is a really great guy.

GEORGIE: We all work with Andrew in unique ways. How do you think you and Andrew work with each other?

ANNA: Well, I don't know if it's unique, but Andrew's just really easy to talk to and he usually gives us an idea of what he wants and then we interpret that and then he'll come back and say yes or that's good or change this. As a director, he allows us a lot of freedom. I'm amazed at how well he works with children. It's great to be working with a director whom I not only trust but admire as a person.

GEORGIE: How do you think audiences will react to the movie?

ANNA: I think it will be well received both by adults who know the book and by children who haven't read it. It will inspire them to read it. It's a really faithful adaptation. It will reach both adults and children on a lot of levels.

INTERVIEW WITH GEORGIE'S DOUBLE, ACTRESS KAYLEIGH CALDWELL

GEORGIE: I'm here with my double, Kayleigh Caldwell. She is the most lovely girl I've ever met. She's bubbly and she's pretty and she's wearing a fantastic necklace, trousers, shoes, and top today and she looks stunning. So, Kayleigh, how do you like working on the movie?

KAYLEIGH: It's been a wonderful experience. I'd love to do it again and again and again.

GEORGIE: Is this your first movie?

KAYLEIGH: Yes, it is, but I've done acting before. And I'd love to be an actress.

GEORGIE: Cool. When's your birthday?

KAYLEIGH: February 15, 1996.

GEORGIE: So you were born in the Year of the Pig? Same here! Cool, thanks for the interview, Kayleigh. It was really nice, and you're a great friend. This is me, Georgie, bye!

Georgie with her stand-in, Kayleigh Caldwell.

TRAVELS WITH GEORGIE: EXCERPTS FROM GEORGIE'S SELF-RECORDED TAPES

Georgie also kept a journal with her recorder, which she took with her wherever she went while making the movie. Here are a few samples.

Hi, this is me, Georgie. I'm in the catering tent; it's Saturday the 18th of September. Today we're going to have a photo shoot, on a Saturday, our day off, but it will be fun. I'm going to get to see the White Witch all made up today for the first time. I'm so excited. I'm guessing that Tilda's going to look great. Skandar says she looks great. Andrew says she looks great. So I hope she looks great. I have to go. Bye.

Hi, this is me, Georgie. I'm here at the lion place where we came to see the lions. We saw a lion called Aslan and his sister was called Narnia. Craig, who's also known as the lion man, got him out of his cage and Andrew and William went up to take a closer look at him. He's a bit of a teenager, and he's very, very moody. Though he's nice.

We saw the white lion cub and his name was Gondor and he was accompanied by another lion cub, called Shakala, though Shakala wasn't a white lion cub. I got licked by Gondor and he had such a rough tongue and he had such blue eyes and such a spacious nose and mouth that he looked like a stuffed toy. It was amazing! They were so cute and we got loads and loads of pictures. When we started to go, the lion was roaring her head off. She just had such a power! We're on our way home now. This is me, Georgie, bye!

Hi, this is me, Georgie. I'm on set and I'm back on the soundstage in Henderson. Whoopee. Today we're going to do the scene where we're watching Edmund go into the White Witch's castle, and I really welly it out. I really shout at Will and Anna, and I'm really dreading that because I don't want to shout at them. And we have to climb up this huge ramp, which is really hard because it's really steep and we keep on falling over because the snow's really thick. I'm just about to get ready, and I'm waiting for Andrea, our dresser, to come and dress me, then I go into makeup and then I go back on set. This is me, Georgie, bye!

ABOVE: *Peter prepares to be knighted.*

OPPOSITE: *The White Witch and Ginarrbrik.*

This is me, Georgie. It's Thursday the 21st of October. Two months until I go back home. I'm traveling out to Muriwai Downs, which is a beautiful location. We're filming the bathing scene with me and Anna in the stream, and we're also filming the scene where William kills Maugrim and Peter gets knighted, so we're going to be doing a lot today. It's cold and sunny. It's going to be even more cold because we're going to be wet so that's not going to be very enjoyable.

Apart from that it's going to be great because we're going to be back with William and Anna!'

This is me, Georgie. It's Friday, the 22nd of October. We just had a splashing fit, me and Anna. I'm running down to the catering tent for lunch. Mission impossible. Mission to get to the catering tent and to have lunch. I have 35 minutes for lunch, which is unusual because I normally have 45 minutes for lunch. I'm running, I'm half-running, half-jogging. I'm entering the catering tent now, and it's very busy and I'm going to have lunch now. This is me, Georgie, bye!

Hi, this is me, Georgie. I've been on the South Island for two days now, and today was our first day of shooting here. It's November 2nd and I went on a magical helicopter ride a few days ago all the way down to Northway Sound and back, which was beautiful. We got out three times. One was at a little stream with these huge mountains over this big lake, the other was on top of a mountain in the snow, and then we got out just to have a breath of fresh air. The scenery here on the South Island is beautiful. We're filming at a place called Oamaru and filming in a lovely place called Elephant Rocks where the rocks are as big as elephants. This is me, Georgie, bye!

AN EPIC CHALLENGE: AN INTERVIEW WITH ANDREW ADAMSON

OPPOSITE: *Andrew Adamson.*

ABOVE: *Production location site.*

After your success with Shrek *, how did you get involved with Narnia?*

I resisted at first. I had read previous scripts with an aim to bid the visual effects when I was a VFX supervisor, but I was never happy with the way they were trying to contemporize the story. So I didn't take the meeting with Walden Media for a long time because I assumed that you would want to do the same thing. It wasn't until my agent, Barbara Dreyfus, said, "Look, they just want to meet with you about a few projects." So I agreed to sit down with you guys.

I remember saying, "Look, if I was even going to do *The Lion, the Witch and the Wardrobe,* here's what I would do." And you all said okay. At that point I thought, maybe I should consider this seriously. And so I re-read the book and thought, "Where's the epic story I remember reading as a child?" The book was much smaller than I remembered it. So I knew the challange was making the movie more three dimensional in terms of scope and characters.

You got hooked on Narnia. What was your biggest challenge?

The big challenge was trying to get to the heart of the characters. I think C. S. Lewis put a lot in there, but he wrote it in a way that was appropriate to children's books of that era. So when you look at Edmund you think, okay, he's a bad boy. But why is he a bad boy? You look at the situation—being in wartime, being sent away from his parents, and Peter becoming the father figure—there are plenty of reasons for Edmund to resent the situation and resent his siblings and therefore betray them. So it was pulling that stuff up to the surface that was a big part of the challenge.

The other challenge was the middle of the book. The second act, if you want to call it that, is a lot of "he-ran, she-ran" as the children are chased. The movie was devoid of action for a very long time. When one of the writers, Ann Peacock, and I first conceived an additional set piece, it was going to be crossing an ice bridge and the ice bridge was melting. That evolved into a Frozen River melting largely because we felt that the idea of the bridge disappearing had happened too many times. I did it in *Shrek* with the dragon and the bridge burning behind them. So I was trying to find something a little more original than that.

What was the most difficult part of researching the movie?

The aesthetics of invented creatures. We tried a lot of forms and proportions. For instance, Centaurs have always intrigued me. I've never seen a successful Centaur and so I wanted to do a Centaur that was aesthetically beautiful. The hard thing about Centaurs is to make the two bodies in proportion. We had to find the correct position of the human hips versus the horse's shoulders so they don't look like a man on a horse. What is fun now is that Rhythm and Hues are using a software program called "Massive," an artificial intelligence where your characters actually have brains that tell them what to do. You tell the characters, okay, you're going to fight some bad guys and the bad guys are going to fight good guys. It's not animated; it's drawn from Motion Capture, which is capturing real motion. In the case of the Centaur, they actually combined the brain of a horse and a person and they basically created a real Centaur so this thing responds as a horse/ person would. When he goes to attack he rears up and uses his legs not his upper body. It's really cool. They showed us some stuff last week. This is a real Centaur; this is how a real Centaur works—by creating a brain that knows about his body. So, it's not guessing

what a move would look like; it's like literally creating a creature.

I remember one time you were doing battle pre-viz and you were talking about the wingspan of the Gryphon.

The creatures must be based in some kind of reality so you imagine what the skeleton of these creatures looks like. When you're talking about a Gryphon, suddenly there's the whole volumetric thing with flying; you have to make sure you have enough wing area to actually support something that large.

Most people don't know that you cut the whole movie and knew exactly what you were going to do before you shot a single frame of film. Tell us a little about the process.

The animatics process is common in animation and less common in live action. In live action you use it a lot for big-effects sequences. Anything that's technically challenging, you storyboard it, adding music, sound effects, voices. Whereas in animation everything is technically difficult, and so you do that for the whole movie. You watch the movie before you make the movie and that way you can iron out problems.

In our case there are things that you think work in script form and then when you put them visually in storyboard form you find redundancies because you're saying things that you're also seeing. Or you watch the whole movie and figure out what scenes you don't need. I did it because I see it as an extension of the writing process. It's a writing tool. And it means that you're not going to have to shoot a lot of wasted stuff. There's only one sequence that we shot that's not in the film: the dance at the coronation.

What were the biggest breakthroughs in the process?

The hardest thing editorially was the pacing between the girls being off with Aslan while the battle was going on. I always felt like the beginning of the battle was undermined by Aslan coming back to life. If Peter knew that Aslan was alive the battle would seem less desperate. It was like that "Charge of the Light Brigade" moment, riding bravely into impossible odds. Even if we withheld the information from Peter, if the audience knows that Aslan is alive, which is the original structure, then it loses that sense of foreboding. So we took the Aslan resurrection that was originally meant to go before the battle and moved it to after the start of the battle.

THIS PAGE AND OPPOSITE: *Conceptual sketches of various creatures of Narnia. Opposite: Oreius the Centaur (top) and a Minotaur (bottom). This page: Gryphons (above) and a Black Dwarf (below).*

Let's talk about working with the kids.

I really wanted to find kids who were close to the characters. And I think in every case I knew immediately who it was going to be when I met them.

William (who plays Peter) is a very good looking boy, but he hadn't done a lot of acting before. Still, he had an incredible openness about him. When I met him, I thought, I would have wanted a big brother like this. He's such a good kid, really

ABOVE: *Andrew and the kids, with Jim Broadbent as Professor Kirke.*

OPPOSITE: *James McAvoy as Tumnus.*

caring. He looked out for the younger kids. I thought that would always come through.

Anna (Susan) was everything the role required: she's smart and kind of sassy and strong, and though she'd hate me to say so, there are many similarities between her and Susan. Anna's a much more patient gentle person than Susan though, and much less of a geek. Apart from being just like Susan, Anna's a wonderful and experienced actor.

I met both Anna and William in the first casting go-around, before I delayed the film for script refinements. I just had to hope they didn't grow too much in the time.

What was so special about Georgie (Lucy) was her capacity for empathy. She instinctively

has the ability to put herself in someone else's shoes. Sometimes it can be difficult for her because she picks up on everyone's moods, but as an actor it's a wonderful ability. It means she's really in the moment, not pretending but really being there, which makes for a very genuine performance.

Skandar (Edmund) was an interesting one because we had almost settled on someone else. The children's casting director, Pippa Hall, brought in a photo of Skandar and he looked so much like an older Georgie—he had these dark mischievous eyes—and I said let's bring him in for the table-read. He was the odd one out because the others knew each other. Georgie kept talking over the top of him and he was getting annoyed and so you could already see some animosity building between them, similar to the characters. We were sold on him right away.

How did you see them grow throughout the course of the movie?

Physically obviously. We shot in chronological order very deliberately because I knew that, one, it would be easier emotionally for the kids and, two, because of their growth. Skandar grew five and a half inches from the time we cast him to the end of the movie and his voice broke in the last couple of months. Georgie grew four inches. William grew about three inches. Anna grew about half an inch.

When did you know they were a family?

Oh, before the shoot. Even when they were hanging out beforehand you could see there was a connection. Even at the early stages of the shoot I remember Georgie feeling a little insecure and going and sitting on William's lap and he gave her a hug. That kind of stuff happened all the time. Right at the beginning, when we were shooting at the

Professor's house, they would goof around together. Skandar would be naughty and knock Georgie over and she'd bump her head and Will would cuddle her and just this great family dynamic evolved.

What about finding some of the other people in the cast?

Tilda was easy. She's just always who I wanted. I loved *Orlando*; it's one of my favorite art house films. I knew the guys who did *The Deep End* and they knew her well. I always thought that physically and intellectually she was right for the part. She was able to pull off cold beauty. One of my big concerns with the witch is that she had become a cliché. When C. S. Lewis wrote her, the character was somewhat original. But others have borrowed his idea. I was conscious of avoiding the cliché. And I knew Tilda would instinctively not go to the cliché. She is too much of an independent thinker.

127

Tell us about James McAvoy as Tumnus.

The Tumnus in the book is a doddery old scholar, and I really didn't want him to be that. Two reasons: you get into the uncomfortable situation with the fact that he takes home an eight-year-old girl and also, again, it seemed like a cliché. Gail Stevens, our casting director, had wanted me to look at James. Although I decided I wanted Tumnus to be handsome and youngish and somebody who immediately exuded warmth and not fear, I felt James was too good-looking and too young. But I watched his performance a couple of times and then Alina Phelan, my assistant, actually made me go back and watch it again. It turned out he was one of the few people who got the double agenda of Tumnus.

Gail had told me that he had deliberately asked her on his first audition not to tell him what I was looking for. He wanted to give me what he thought the character was. He had grown up on this story. So we went to London to meet with him and I realized he was Scottish. I had no idea. His accent on the tape was so English; he completely caught me by surprise. He arrived on his motorcycle on an early Sunday morning. He always just got that character. Then the thing that I could never have hoped for or anticipated was how much he developed a kinship with Georgie—they genuinely liked each other. They would goof around between takes. That's so important to the role. And they would do Posh and Beckham. You would hear them between takes doing their little skits. Georgie would just get so excited when he'd come back for a scene. That connection comes through on the screen.

When James would do scenes where he was scared, it would take Georgie a day to recover because she was so genuinely upset by seeing James upset. One bit when he's saying good-bye to her the first time they meet, he chokes up; Georgie says, "Hey, hey," to comfort him. She wasn't conscious of acting in that moment. That happened a lot. They just had this great connection.

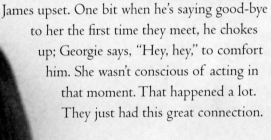

Did you ever have any moments when you were shooting when you felt magic was happening?

A lot of moments. When we saw William riding a horse and just seeing him become a young warrior; those moments on the Stone Table with Anna. One of the most sublime images in the film is one where Anna's finished crying and she's just watching Georgie cry and there's such sympathy and empathy in her face. When Tumnus and Lucy say good-bye, there's this wonderful, genuine sadness between James and Georgie. And then Skandar, the scene where he goes to the White Witch's castle. He was great. Where she says, "How dare you . . ." and he asks "Can I have more Turkish Delight now?" It's such a great turn for Tilda and him both.

Do you have a favorite location?

I really liked the elephant rocks on Oamaru at Aslan's camp. I always sensed that it was very peaceful, this strangely serene place where we shot Aslan's camp. I liked it a lot more before we filmed it with a thousand people. And I liked it when we were just checking on stuff after the crew had left and Aslan's camp was empty. It's a strangely spiritual place. Interestingly enough, it's called Whale Bone because they found whale bones in the rocks. When you walk in there, you start talking in a hushed voice. That's a place I would go back to.

If you had one scene to reshoot, which would it be?

I would like to reshoot the girls watching Aslan die. Because we shot that in a tent in sixty-mile-an-hour winds and it was very, very hard to get them into the right head space.

Who's your favorite bad-guy creature?

My favorite bad-guy creature is probably Otmin. He's pretty cool, formidable. My assistant had a crush on him. Not on the actor playing him—on Otmin the Minotaur.

What about your favorite good-guy creature?

The good-guy creatures are hard. I love the Centaurs. As a character I like Tumnus as the best good guy. And Mr. Beaver's a great guy. The coolest looking good-guy creature is the Gryphon.

Which visual effect are you most proud of?

Aslan is astounding. From the beginning I wanted him to be completely photo real. The reason C. S. Lewis used a lion is the awe and fear it inspires. It's both attractive and repulsive. You want to approach a lion but you know it can bite your head off. And that's a very Old Testament, God-like image—this idea of somebody that's both awe inspiring and fear inspiring. I wanted to make sure that our lion conveyed all of that in a believable way. That you never find yourself thinking, "Wow. Great CG lion," loving only the character.

Let's talk about the voice actors who play the characters.

In some cases you know exactly who you're going to go out to. I had just finished working with

OPPOSITE: *Elephant Rocks.*

RIGHT: *Otmin the Minotaur, Andrew Adamson's favorite bad guy.*

Jennifer Saunders as the Fairy Godmother in *Shrek 2,* and so I was thinking of her comedy partner Dawn French for the part of Mrs. Beaver. As soon as we started listening to voices, hers was the one that leapt out.

With Mr. Beaver I wanted a down-to-earth quality. I always thought Mr. Beaver was a real blue-collar guy—down to earth, good, funny, hard working, and tough. Ray Winstone has all of that in his voice. When casting voices, I close my eyes to the video or just listen to them on audio tape. Sometimes you can be fooled by the physical performance. Ray definitely has a voice that could carry everything Mr. Beaver had to do, a lot of which was to deliver exposition in a disarming way.

How did you cast the Fox?

I was actually doing the junket in Cannes for *Shrek 2* and I saw Rupert Everett there. Rupert just said, "I have to be in your movie; you have to put me in your movie; I love that book." And I said, "Strangely I hadn't thought of a part for you," just because he was Prince

131

Charming for me in *Shrek 2*. And then I thought, "Oh, I have a part of a Fox if you're interested." And I think he just made the deal on the spot. I think he called up his agent and said he wanted to do it. Didn't even read the material or anything. And we recorded it a week later on his way back from Cannes.

How did you find the voice of Aslan?

Aslan was a great challenge: finding the voice that had the depth and the resonance I wanted and to be somewhat accent-less. That you wouldn't hear the voice and go, "Oh that's so and so playing Aslan." I wanted the actor to disappear in the part. The nice thing with Liam Neeson is the fact that he is Irish but he played his accent down. You can't really pick where he's from, and he has this great resonance and warmth. Which at the same time it can get angry and strong in a moment, like where he yells at the White Witch. And then on top of all that he can be very gentle and warm and paternal. He was great. It's a difficult character and Liam completely believed in him.

Tell us about Michael Madsen as Maugrim, the Wolf Captain of the White Witch's secret police.

Michael was a late addition. Our producer, Mark Johnson, brought up Michael because he'd worked with him before. I don't know why he hadn't occurred to us earlier. Again, Mark just called him up and said, "I'm doing this film, are you interested?" and he said, "Sure," and showed up and did it. He was great. He has this fantastic voice, a good bad guy. He was really funny. I started showing him some tapes and he's like, "I get it, I'm a wolf."

How did you come to choose Sim Evan Jones as your editor?

Sim had done *Shrek* and *Shrek 2* with me. He was familiar with the animatic process. Not every editor knows how to cut that stuff and make it work. He's used to dealing with sound design that paints in between the pictures. When you've got only fifteen storyboard panels to work with in a scene, you've got to fill in all this richness of texture with sound. He's used to doing that. On top of that, we just have a very similar aesthetic.

Our other film editor was Jim May. Jim's main experience was as an effects editor. This is one of the first films he had done as a full-on editor. He's proved to be invaluable in both of those areas. Early on he would cut sequences and he'd show them to Sim; then he'd show them to me. I'd give my comments and he'd say Sim had exactly the same comments.

The thing that Sim brings to all of his projects is his music sensibility. It's something we've always had in common. This may be one of the best "temp" scores we've ever heard. In *Shrek* I was a lot more involved with the music. On this one I've let Sim kind of run off and do more and just show me stuff. More that nine times out of ten it's been exactly on the money.

Let's talk about music. How did Harry Gregson-Williams come to be in the project?

Harry scored both *Shrek* films. One of the things I always respected about him is his willingness to try new things. You can't listen to a movie and go, "That's probably a Harry Gregson-Williams score." A lot of composers, like authors, have developed a certain style and Harry I've always found to be very flexible. In this movie I didn't want it to have just that classic orchestral epic movie sound. I wanted to find a different music unique to Narnia and I thought he would be capable of doing that.

How did you two come up with the song Tumnus plays to lull Lucy to sleep?

I love that piece of music, but it's always a similar process. Harry gets very frustrated because he tries three or four passes and I just keep saying no and trying to articulate exactly what it is I do or don't like about it. In that one I felt it was too Celtic. I called him and said, "Can we start exploring different ethnicities of music?" I was thinking about Middle Eastern music or Turkish music or something like that. And then he will tell me why I'm thinking that. It's a certain timing or a certain key. He's very good at understanding and then being able to articulate technically what that is. On about the fourth or fifth try about two days before we shot that, he sent this piece that I thought was just perfect.

We'd been doing the scene several times with James and Georgie where he'd just be blowing the flute, which sounded like a recorder. Then we set up the speakers and we didn't tell Georgie. James got to the bit and he went to blow and Harry's music came on. Georgie's face was fantastic. We couldn't actually use it because then she just cracked up laughing.

What was the process collaborating with the C. S. Lewis Company, the creative partnership with Doug Gresham?

It was always great. It was one of the things that I was very afraid of when I got involved with the project. Estates can be difficult, particularly when you're going from book to screen. You can be faithful to the themes and you can be faithful to the scenes and characters and everything but you have to make changes because what works in book form doesn't necessarily work on film. And when people from an estate have lived with something for years and years it's sometimes hard for them to understand those changes. We were mainly dealing with Doug on a creative level; he knows the material very well, and he was always open to

OPPOSITE: *Conceptual sketch of Maugrim.*

ABOVE: *Andrew and Douglas Gresham.*

BELOW: *Andrew and the kids.*

debate. He was always willing to discuss any idea and be convinced or not or to stress why I needed to address something particularly for historical or theological reasons.

How do you address the religious implications of the text?

While I wanted a film that was for everyone, I didn't want to take out of it anything that had spiritual implications. I wanted to make sure that the people who got a spiritual message from the book were able to get the same from the movie as well. On the other hand, I wanted it to be accessible to everyone to the point of view that if you enjoyed the book as an adventure, or merely like this kind of movie, then you'll enjoy the movie as a great adventure and family drama.

What are you most proud of about this movie?

I guess I'm most proud of the fact that I like it. I know that sounds strange. But with a movie that's this complex technically and story-wise and with it being an adaptation that's true to an original book and true to an image and a memory that a lot of people share, there are many opportunities to fail. So I am proud that it is a good movie.

I'm also proud of the kids. I don't just mean I'm simply proud of our work together. I'm genuinely proud of them as if they were my kids that went out and did a good job on something.

What do you want audiences to take away or feel when they leave the theater?

I want children to feel empowered. I think that's what the book did for kids more than

anything else. That's why it's universally appealing to children. They go from being in this world where they're treated as children—they're being pushed around and disenfranchised and fragmented as a family by World War II. And they go into a land where they are no longer referred to as children; they're kings and queens, and they are ultimately the thing that's going to save this land. They go from being children to warriors and that's such an empowering story for children.

I also want families to take away from it, other than an enjoyable experience, a sense of what a family is, a sense of unity and sticking together, of supporting each other. It's a story of betrayal and forgiveness; Edmund betrays Peter; Peter and the others have a hard time forgiving him for that betrayal. You've got two girls separated by their ages; the older one has to learn how to be a child again; the younger has to learn to grow up a little bit so they can meet in the middle. So, ultimately, I think there's a story of family in there, a family that is empowered through their unity. Those are the main things I want people to take away from the film.

And then if I had to say what the one message for the film is, what the one theme was in the book that I wanted to put in the film, it is that of forgiveness. I think that's the most important message.

So what's next?

Nothing. A rest.

135

MAKING NARNIA
A REAL PLACE:
ROGER FORD AND
THE PRODUCTION
DESIGN TEAM

FOR A GUY WHO NEVER read the book as a kid, production designer Roger Ford knocked this movie out of the park. "When I got the call about designing the film, I had to confess I'd missed out on reading it as a child. So I bought a copy and, that evening while I was reading it, my son Oliver, who's now twenty-seven, came around. I told him about the great book I'd just bought. Then he said, 'Dad, we've got all seven Narnia books on the bookshelf. Mum used to read them to me all the time.' So that was my introduction to the story."

"The book is about imagination," Roger explains. "So the imagery is provided by a child's and the reader's imagination. It's the magic of the book, and the best kids' books leave it to the reader. So that's what we have to deal with. The scenery is often better in the book, because it's created in your imagination.

"It's daunting," Roger continues, because "you have to surprise the audience. You have to delight them. You've got to go further than their

imagination takes them. It's not an easy thing to do."

The research phase of development was aided by Roger's early memories. The opening segment of the film is set in a London suburb during the Blitzkrieg, which Roger lived through: "I remember as a very small child in bed at night, hearing the bombers fly over the house. It was terrifying.

"The children are at the Professor's house by page two in the book. Because what happened during World War II means very little to our audience nowadays, Andrew

OPPOSITE: *Edmund discovers Narnia.*

ABOVE: *The Stone Table location set.*

RIGHT: *Production designer Roger Ford.*

extended the part of the story where the children are evacuated from the city to the country. Credibility at the beginning of the film was essential. If we couldn't be totally believable about wartime London and the circumstances of the time, then we'd lose the audience very quickly.

"So we figured out the Professor lived somewhere near the Welsh border, somewhere west. Where did trains go from London to the west? Paddington Station. Which company ran the trains? The Great Western Railway. Then we found in the Severn Valley Railway in the U.K. some of the old Great Western carriages and engines, restored and still running. We built part of Platform One, Paddington Station, in the studio. We built the train carriage to match the ones at the Severn Valley Railway. Then we went to the U.K. to film the shots of the train on location.

"We tried to build up a believable England before we moved into Narnia. And then Andrew wanted Narnia, in its own way, to be equally believable, not a fantasy world."

Andrew set a high standard for the movie: Narnia had to be a real world. And that's what they made. "A lot of our early work," Roger says, "went into how to achieve snow that would convince a child, because most children know what snow is all about—falling snow, footprints in the snow. A lot of tests went into that. Then we embellished that with some shots of real snow in the Czech Republic and hoped it would all come together."

They worked hard for the same realism in building Mr. and Mrs. Beaver's dam. "There's an excellent documentary on the way beavers build their dams, and there's even a shot from inside the beavers' house of a bear trying to get in," Roger recalls. "And it's ripping away these sticks and dried mud. Of course, we've got the same image in our film with the Wolves trying to get into the Beavers' house." This painstaking realism elevates the movie above average fantasy.

Part of the reason Roger made it look both believable and beautiful was the expert cinematography of Don McAlpine, the director of photography. The haunting interiors of the White Witch's castle are a majestic highlight of their artistic harmony.

"In the book, the Witch's castle is not described as being made of ice," Roger says. "We made a creative decision early on that we would build the castle out of ice, and that all seemed very exciting at the time, but then of course comes the problem of how to create the 'ice.' Don did a fantastic job lighting it to help it look like real ice. We had a very good working relationship."

Sometimes Roger took a detail from the original text and expanded it in the design. For instance, C. S. Lewis described the Narnian castle Cair Paravel as being decorated with peacock feathers. "Now in the book, it feels as if that means actual peacock feathers around the hall. But Pauline Baynes's illustration in the book has the peacock feathers printed on the fabric behind the thrones. So, like her, we ran with the idea of a decorative motif. We always thought stained glass windows behind the thrones would give a lovely lighting opportunity. The design is based on peacock feathers. We've got the motif recurring throughout Cair Paravel, even in some of the floor patterns."

The entire art department paid meticulous attention to Andrew's vision. Andrew found the inspiration for Tumnus's house in the Czech Republic, for instance, in a natural setting, a crevice nestled tightly in a dazzling rock formation. It was then up to Roger's team to recreate the exact natural setting in the studio, "so one of our plasterers, coming from the U.K., stopped in the Czech Republic on his way to New Zealand and took what is called a "squeeze," which means an impression, a mold of the rock, and he brought it to Auckland with him. Then when we put our rocks together on set, we have rocks identical in texture to the ones we'll be shooting later (for the exterior shots) on location in the Czech Republic."

The art department boasted the biggest number of people on the movie. The construction jobs were enormous. Art director Ian Gracie made sure all these glorious designs actually became a reality—and on schedule. Roger describes him simply as "up there with the best in the world." Also indispensable was set decorator Kerrie Brown, whom Roger had worked with for many years.

One of their biggest construction jobs on the movie was creating Lantern Waste on a soundstage in New Zealand—a snowy forested area with a giant lamp-post growing out of the ground. The

ABOVE: *The director of photography, Don McAlpine.*

OPPOSITE: *Exterior of Tumnus's house.*

problem was finding a structure big enough and high enough to take the scale of Narnia forests that Andrew wanted. The solution: grab a shovel and dig. "It was an equestrian center," explains Roger; "but the advantage of it was that it had an earth floor. Normally, you have to build everything up from the concrete floor. At the Kelly Park Equestrian Center, about an hour outside Auckland, we were able to dig down six or seven meters below floor level and so create our landscape. Then we put in two or three hundred trees. There's a huge tree farming industry in New

Zealand," Roger adds. "So we used mostly farmed trees, especially conifers."

Once the forest was built, there was the small affair of adding the finishing touches, namely snow and a lamp-post. "The snow came in from the U.K. in container loads," Roger says, "from a company called 'Snow Business' who have developed a range of very good fake snow products."

Next came the famous lamp-post, part of the original image that came to C. S. Lewis when he was young and that inspired the book. "We brought in the lamp-post from the U.K.," Roger explains. "It's a casting of an original Victorian London lamp-post. We obtained the proper gas fitting. There's a beautiful shot in the film looking down through the lamp-post with the flickering flames in the foreground. "The Narnian lamp-post grows from the lamp-post the Witch throws in *The Magician's Nephew*, the prequel to *The Lion, the Witch and the Wardrobe*. In London the Witch uses the lamp-post to beat everyone up with. So when she is whisked off to Narnia, she throws it away into the forest, and it grows. Andrew's idea was to have some sort of roots around the bottom of it, not woody roots, but cast iron roots. It's very subtle, you'll have to look carefully to see them, but they're there. The lamp-post has actually grown in the forest." It's the perfect blend of magic and realism.

Everyone has a favorite set. For Don McAlpine it's inside the White Witch's castle during the brilliantly lit dungeon sequence. For me, it's the White Witch's courtyard, her statue garden, stone sculptures of her enemies and brave Narnians who dared to defy her. Originally, the courtyard posed another problem for production design: Roger Ford had to worry about filling it.

"I imagined when we started," Roger explains, "huge numbers of sculptures of stone creatures, all sorts of creatures who had been turned to stone by the White Witch. There are Giant Bears, Centaurs, Giants, and so on. During preproduction

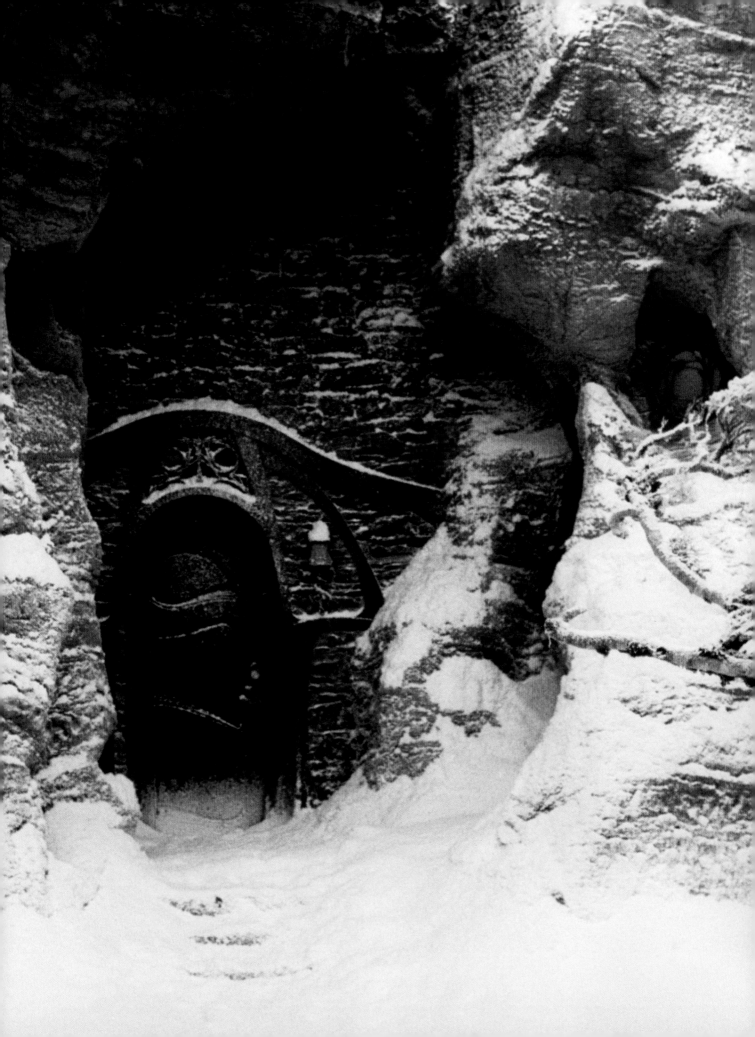

I was thinking how long does it take someone to sculpt lifelike creatures like that? How are we ever going to get so many sculptures?"

Well, he got them. Thanks in large part to John Searle, the head sculptor, who led a group of artists who individually sculpted each and every statue in the movie.

"I'd have to say my favorite was Rumblebuffin, the four-meter giant," Searle says. "I suppose it was purely his size and the character we were able to portray that made it so rewarding to see him standing frozen in time in the Queen's courtyard. Second to him would have to have been the pair of rearing Gryphon, half lion/half bird of prey."

That set still takes my breath away. It was also my favorite image from the book, mysterious and fantastic. But Andrew, Roger, and John and his team did one better than my mind's eye. They made it real.

Andrew always had a wonderful vision for color as it plays out in the movie. He tracked the

story through its evolution of color; it's one of the fundamental reasons the movie pleases on such a visual level.

"The beginning of the film is somber in color," says Roger Ford. "It's mostly gray and rainy, even at the Professor's house. The next part of the film in Narnia is almost monochromatic, almost black and white, the silhouettes of the trees against the snow, even the children in their fur coats.

"But then as spring comes," Roger explains, "so does more color. We introduce flowers into the landscape." You can track the seasons throughout the movie—another essential idea from Andrew's original conception. Each season is reflected in the set design: Narnia begins in winter, spring arrives with Aslan, the coronation takes place during summer, and the children, having grown into the autumn of their reign, chase the White Stag through the burnt-colored leaves of the forest in fall.

"Roger was inspired by a neoclassical look for Cair Paravel, and I loved it when he told me what he wanted," remembers costume designer Isis Mussenden. "I thought it was a beautiful idea, full of light and alabaster and joy. It was perfect, all the flowers and colors, how you could dress with it. We got to lighten it up."

"The illustrations in the book suggest that it's a medieval castle," Roger says of Cair Paravel. "But I thought, we're in Narnia after all, we're not in England anymore. It is its own world, and it has its own time frame. So after studying a lot of rather somber and dark medieval castles, cathedrals, and churches, we came to the decision with Andrew to lighten up Cair Paravel. So we started looking at neoclassical paintings that were washed with sunlight and gentle color, often Mediterranean in feel, and usually based in antiquity. We started to think of Cair Paravel as a light-filled palace of celebration and joy."

Production design involves more than just building different architectural structures. For one thing, the group had to convince us that all the ice in the movie was real. This became especially tricky with the sequence on the Frozen River. Andrew conceived the idea early on that the film needed an additional scene at midpoint to create a heightened moment of peril for the children that would also mirror the midpoint in their own character struggles. It takes place as the children cross a Frozen River at the bottom of a Frozen Waterfall. Since spring is coming, the Waterfall is starting to burst through the ice, and the ice is starting to crack. What could make things worse? This is where the Wolves catch up with them.

Roger Ford began with intense research on the natural phenomenon of frozen waterfalls. "There's lots of reference you can get from photographs of frozen waterfalls," he says. "They're beautiful looking things with huge icicles and mounds of snow." To achieve the look of water suddenly bursting through the ice, they built the floor of the set with sheets of foam covered in fiberglass, wax, and paint.

"When you walked on it," Roger says, "I have to say it looked amazingly like ice. And because the ice had cracked we designed each segment, each cracked piece of ice, and then the effects department put each segment on hydraulic rams."

OPPOSITE TOP: *Conceptual sketch for the lamp-post.*

OPPOSITE BOTTOM: *Doug Gresham poses as a size reference for the stone Rumblebuffin.*

ABOVE: *Susan, Lucy, and Peter cross the Frozen River.*

They rigged it so that the hydraulics reacted to weight. As soon as the actors stepped on them, the ice segments would move. "And they had water hoses underneath," Roger adds, "coming up and squirting up through the cracks as the ice moved." The reaction from the young actors was genuine surprise: they'd step on the wrong piece of ice and it would suddenly move! "Quite disconcerting," Roger says, "but really very effective."

There is so much meaning in every set in the movie, but even with the movie finally done, there's still a question about one small, significant design detail. What do the ancient words carved around the Stone Table mean?

"Well that's a bit of a mystery," Roger Ford says. "I think you should ask Aslan that."

Roger Ford also had the challenging job of determining what the famous wardrobe actually looked like. "Well, that was a major project," he sighs. "I mean, it's probably the most important prop in the film."

Of course Andrew came up with something special for it. Andrew isn't a fan of just *The Lion, the Witch and the Wardrobe*, he's a fan of the whole *Chronicles of Narnia*. The minute he started the job, he began researching the origins of the book. He dove into the prequel, *The Magician's Nephew*, which ironically C. S. Lewis wrote years after the first volume. Fascinated by the explanations and origins of everything that appears in *The Lion, the Witch and the Wardrobe*—from the lamp-post to the wardrobe itself—Andrew decided to tell the story of *The Magician's Nephew* through the detailed wood carvings on the front of the wardrobe.

If you look closely, you can see the entire story play out. It's the perfect wink-and-a-nod to fans everywhere.

Conceptual painting for Cair Paravel's throne room.

THE RINGS
(top-right corner)

The magical green and yellow rings that transport the wearer to and from the Wood between the Worlds.

THE WOOD BETWEEN THE WORLDS
(directly below it, on the right-hand side)

The timeless forest between worlds, characterized by pools of water everywhere.

CHARN
(directly below that, on the right-hand side)

The ruined city, a cruel and warlike civilization left cold and silent by the bitter power struggle between Jadis and her sister, the Empress. Jadis ultimately destroyed it when she uttered the Deplorable Word.

THE GOLDEN BELL
(directly below, bottom-right corner)

Young Digory, against his friend Polly's better judgment, follows the writings on the wall in the royal hall of Charn and with the hammer rings the enchanted bell, whose clang awakens Jadis and triggers an earthquake that destroys the still city.

THE FIRST SUNRISE
(center bottom)

Aslan sings Narnia into existence, and the sun rises with it.

FLEDGE, THE WINGED HORSE
(bottom-left corner)

Originally the cab-horse named Strawberry who is transported from London to Narnia. When Aslan sings Narnia into existence, he transforms Strawberry into a beautiful winged horse, who carries Digory and Polly to the garden.

OPPOSITE: *The wardrobe.*

NEXT PAGES: *The kids at Aslan's camp.*

THE GARDEN ON TOP OF THE HILL
(above that, left-hand side)

Aslan sends Digory to pick the Silver Apple from inside the faraway garden of the West, which sits on top of a steep, green hill, whose gates face the rising sun.

THE BIRD IN THE TREE
(above that, left-hand side)

When Digory is taking the Silver Apple from the tree in the garden on top of the hill, he notices a wonderful, exotic bird watching him and decides against taking an apple for himself.

THE APPLE
(above that, upper-left corner)

There are two apples of note in *The Magician's Nephew*. First is the Silver Apple that Aslan commands Digory to get from the garden of the West. When Digory returns, Aslan has him plant the apple and from it grows the Tree of Protection, which keeps the White Witch out of Narnia for a time. Digory picks an apple from this new tree, and when he brings it home and gives it to his dying mother, the magic apple cures her.

TWO CROWNS
(top center)

The two crowns symbolize the coronation of King Frank and Queen Helen, the first king and queen of Narnia.

THE APPLE TREE
(center)

After Digory feeds his mother the apple from Narnia and it heals her, he buries the core in his backyard. This magnificent apple tree springs from it. Years later, when a gale finally blows down the tree, Digory can't bear to have it chopped up, so he had part of the timber made into a very special wardrobe that Lucy Pevensie would one day discover in *The Lion, the Witch and the Wardrobe*.

THE WONDERFUL WORLD OF WETA

By Ben Wootten, Richard Taylor, and Weta Workshop

THE WETA WORKSHOP TEAM HAD JUST finished *The Lord of the Rings*. The question on everybody's mind was, "Where do we go from here?" Then we heard a quiet murmur: "Somebody is making *The Lion, the Witch and the Wardrobe* into a movie," and then, "It might be coming to New Zealand—we may be working on it." All of this was confirmed on September 2, 2002.

Richard Taylor met with director Andrew Adamson at a café in L.A. just down the road from Disney. The last time Richard had seen Andrew was ten years ago as Richard applied skull make-up to Andrew before a party celebrating reaching the halfway point on Peter Jackson's *The Frighteners*. At the time, Andrew had been assisting Weta Digital with the visual effects of the film. Now Andrew wanted to discuss his intention to adapt *The Lion, the Witch and the Wardrobe* for the screen. For Weta Workshop to have been offered the opportunity to bring one much-loved piece of English literature to the screen with *The Lord of the Rings* was an incredible opportunity, but to now be offered a chance to explore Narnia as well was beyond belief.

Due to the intense workload the company was already undertaking, the team realized at a very early stage that Weta Workshop would not be able to undertake the sort of involvement that it had on *The Lord of the Rings*. We would need to share the work with others. This afforded the wonderful opportunity to work alongside Richard's close friend Howard Berger and his team from KNB EFX Group.

Andrew is a great visual director and quickly began to outline the land of Narnia in broad strokes through regular videoconference calls. Andrew also had a great relationship with Walden Media,

OPPOSITE: *Cyclops at Aslan's camp.*

LEFT: *Axe, courtesy of Weta.*

the production team making the film. In fact, executive producer Perry Moore was a C. S. Lewis enthusiast and mythology buff, and a great ally for the creative team at Weta and KNB. Armed with the descriptions from the director, Weta began to explore the world.

The first steps were the hardest. We needed a world no one had seen before, but Narnia was not "new." It was an old world, well known to millions of readers. Also, in the wake of *The Lord of the Rings*, Weta's designers were eager to ensure that Narnia's design would be fresh and distinct.

The Weta Design Team, led by Richard Taylor and Ben Wootten, began what would be a journey of discovery and wonder. First, the creatures were to be explored. Whereas Tolkien had created an alternate universe, self-contained and with as full and compete a history as our own, C. S. Lewis had made a land linked to ours. Through a wardrobe door, the children discover a magical land filled with strange creatures plucked from our own mythology—Minotaurs, Unicorns, Centaurs, Fauns. These creatures had been with humankind since the days of ancient Greece. So was Weta to stay with established looks or find fresh takes on old ideas?

It soon become obvious to both Andrew and us that there would be little point in trying to reinvent the wheel, so to speak. When the children of the story stepped through the wardrobe, they were stepping into a child's dream state, where ordinary rules did not apply. The design parameters were much broader than, say, Middle Earth's. This was a fundamental appreciation the design team came to: we would design familiar creatures visualized as realistically as the concept allowed, but dressed and behaving as they had never been seen to do so on film previously. A depth of character and culture would define a Narnian Centaur from all Centaurs seen before.

Early conceptions for the Minotaur, Centaur, and Maugrim.

Weekly one- to two-hour video conferences between L.A. and Wellington involved discussions of the last week's drawings and sculpture, and each time the designs were brought a step closer to the final designs as seen on the screen. As the different races took shape, the questions of culture, physiology, and lifestyle became as important as the look of the creatures themselves. The design flowed naturally onto the armor and weapons. Having come to know the creatures so well by this point, it was readily apparent, to the designers, how they would move and behave. For instance, a Minotaur wore armor mainly on his front. He would never retreat. His heavy body armor was made of plate steel but left his powerful legs free so as not to impede mobility. This intimate knowledge and thought was brought to bear on all of the races.

Because the creatures were going to be realized digitally in the final film, the next step was to create "scannable maquettes." These were large, detailed sculptures. Where the design maquettes were quick three-dimensional sketches, taking one to two days each, the scannable maquettes were highly detailed, fully finished pieces, created to serve as the ultimate reference for digital models. Form and function were as important as surface detail—these sculptures had to be anatomically correct from the inside out. Contained in any one of these sculpts would have to be all the information digital effects company Rhythm & Hues would need to bring the creatures to life in their computers.

The scannable maquettes also offered the designers a chance to review the designs, seen in

RIGHT: *Minotaur armor.*

BELOW: *Scannable Minotaur maquette.*

larger, more finished, forms. Andrew fine-tuned the proportions and subtle features to find his perfect vision for each race.

The Centaurs benefited most from this part of the process; the four-foot (1.2m) sculptures allowed Weta's designers to explore and find the best balance between the human and horse components of this handsome race.

Each sculpt was then molded and reproduced in urethane for shipping to the United States, where they would begin their journey into the digital realm. The sad part was that most were missing their hair or feathers as these features would be added digitally later. The sight of a plucked Phoenix was not a noble one—the proud bird looked more like a store-bought chicken.

In all Weta produced twelve scannable maquettes, each taking about four to six weeks of sculpting time—among them, Aslan, a Minotaur, a Mermaid, and a Faun.

The weapons were produced as life-size cardboard cutouts so we could assess the size and look of a weapon and its feel in the hands of its final owner. Questions such as "Is that scimitar too big for a Faun?" or "Is the head of the Minotaur's axe too small?" could not be answered until seen in the hands or claws of the appropriately sized character.

Then there was the issue of manufacturing the armor. Form and function became the all-encompassing issues here. Drawing a cool suit of armor was all very well, but whether somebody could wear and perform in it was another story entirely. We relied heavily on the experienced Weta "on-set" technicians who knew how well

ABOVE: *A Centaur model.*

BELOW: *Centaur sword.*

OPPOSITE: *An armored Centaur.*

any given armor design would actually work. The true functionality of the item would dictate any necessary adjustments to the final look— a breastplate might get narrower to accommodate a performer's proportions between the shoulders, a sword handle longer and heavier to balance the blade. This feedback into the design would strengthen it, adding to the realism and familiarity that defined the difference between a great looking, real suit and a whimsical, obviously made-up suit of fantasy armor.

When making weaponry or armor for a movie, our approach has always been to do so as if making the real thing—but this was not always possible. Where possible, metal armor was hand-beaten and acid-etched, and swords were ground from high-grade steel and finished with wood and leather. Swordsmith Peter Lyon and blacksmith Stu Johnson attacked this job with fervor. The reason for this approach could be seen when these items were silicon molded and reproduced in large numbers for use on set. Each reproduction had the look and handmade finish of the originals, having retained the textures inherent in the hand-making process. The beautifully finished hero steel armor and weapons could also be used for close-up work and never seem at odds with the rest.

Where the standard method of manufacture was not possible, a more eclectic form of prop making was employed. Custom-board, lead, car filler, and plasticine could be used by a skilled model maker to produce beautifully detailed and realistic looking items. Weta's senior prop makers John Harvey and Callum Lingard, in conjunction with Richard Taylor and workshop supervisor

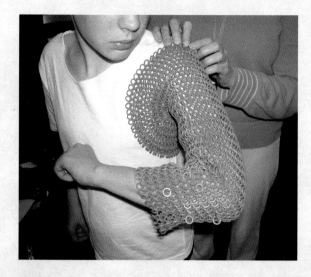

We also made extensive use of new hi-tech equipment. A laser-cutter played the midfield on many items produced for this film. Whereas on previous films much of the design work was translated into etch screens and leather stamps by hand, such pattern work could now be cut straight into the desired material directly from the design drawings. Another impressive piece of new equipment was a 3-D printer. A very sophisticated piece of digitally driven hardware, this machine could print an object three dimensionally from a file at practically any scale—the perfect tool for prototyping highly complex, but exacting sculptural shapes like sword hilts and such.

Another major advancement was a type of chain-mail manufacturing developed on *The Lord of the Rings*, but improved upon since then. This Weta-designed chain mail was created out of thousands of linked plastic rings, but where in the past it had been sliced from lengths of plastic pipe, for *The Lion, the Witch and the Wardrobe*, each ring was an individually cast item, specially produced for creating realistic, replica chain mail. Partnered with friend and colleague Fred Tang, the company could now produce custom chain mail. This allowed veteran Carl Payne to pattern beautiful suits of chain armor for Narnia's kings, Peter and Edmund, not to mention the host of other characters on the battlefield.

Overall Weta Workshop designed and produced a significant number of weapons and suits of armor. We used a range of different materials to cater to the huge variety of uses required of props on set—steel for close-up hero shots and aluminum-bladed weapons for mid-ground characters or safe fighting. Aircraft aluminum was used for these weapons as it is strong and durable but, above all, light. Swinging a sword around was dangerous work. This might be all well and good in a war, but on the film set, actors may be needed to survive a day's shooting in one piece, so safety was always a concern.

TOP: *Edmund being fitted with chain-mail sleeve.*

ABOVE: *Edmund in full armor.*

OPPOSITE: *Edmund battles with a Dwarf.*

Jason Docherty, determined what methods would produce the best results—the Minotaurs' armor, for example, was made by sculpting the fine relief detail in plasticine over metal forms. Repeating details were sculpted once and reproduced to set into the finished sculpt. Once molded and cast in a urethane compound, the painted result was a beautiful, finely crafted suit of seemingly hand-beaten armor.

Urethane-bladed weapons were created for background characters as they were cheaper to produce in numbers and very durable.

One of the interesting complications that Weta Workshop had not run into before was the age of the young cast and the growth spurts they were going through. The problem with steel (and even chain-mail armor, to an extent) was that it didn't allow any give and thus had to be specifically tailored to fit a performer. As the boys shot up in height over the course of the project, it became necessary to adjust and rebuild their armor. Components had to be rebuilt and altered to compensate for their swiftly changing frames. Weta Workshop's on-set team—Tim Tozer, Rob Gillies,

Joe Dunckley, and Simon Hall—quickly gained a reputation for hard work and enthusiastic effort, something the team back in the Workshop in Wellington was proud to hear of.

The two and half years that we spent on *The Lion, the Witch and the Wardrobe* were enjoyable. Not only did we have the opportunity to share in bringing another wonderful piece of English literature to the screen, but also we got to collaborate with an amazing group of filmmakers, helmed by fellow New Zealander Andrew Adamson. Andrew's astute eye and calm yet enthusiastic demeanor made him a pleasure to work with. The whole filmmaking experience was a wonderful one with his great strength of vision.

CREATURE FEATURE: NARNIA'S TALKING BEASTS

By Howard Berger, Head Creature Designer and Supervisor

IN JUNE 2003 MY GOOD FRIEND RICHARD Taylor, the owner of Weta Workshop in New Zealand, called to say he had recommended my makeup effects company, KNB EFX Group, to handle the creation of the characters his workshop had conceptualized for the upcoming movie version of *The Lion, the Witch and the Wardrobe*. This was the show I'd been waiting for during the past twenty-three years of my professional life. My wife, Sandi, and my children, Kelsey, Travis, and Jacob, were likewise fans of the book and assured me that I was the best person for the job.

When I first met Andrew Adamson, the director, at his modest production office in Burbank, he showed me the presentation room, where hundreds of preproduction drawings for the

Narnia movie hung. These drawings by the preproduction artists were presented in the order of the film as Andrew envisioned it. I was overwhelmed by the detailed thought he had put into this project already. We then walked into another room that housed the maquettes (small study sculptures) that Weta had produced to demonstrate possible creature concepts in 3-D.

Then Andrew sat me down and we watched his early version of the animatics of the final battle, where the majority of the creatures would play. I was so touched by what I saw that I blurted out, "That was amazing. I *have* to work on this film!"

When Richard Taylor was working on *The Lord of the Rings* films, I would go down to New Zealand to visit him, and he always spoke about the characters and places in the films as if they were

ARCHERS   MEDIUM   OERIUS   HEAVY   HORSE   UNICORN   REINDEER   WHITE STAG   BEAR   RHINOCEROUS   WILD BOAR   FOX   GREAT DOG   LEOPARD   CHEETAH   LIONESS
      CENTAURS   BIG CATS

real to him. In my dedicated work on over four hundred films, I had never "believed" to the extent that Richard and the Weta gang had believed in Middle Earth. Well, I knew that this film would be different: we would be designing and building not *creatures,* but *Narnians.* I wanted everyone at KNB—all 120 craftsmen and -women working alongside me—to feel and believe that this was a real place and these were real living beasts in the land.

When I got the call from Andrew awarding KNB the show in January 2004, I was in heaven. I called my kids immediately and said, "We're going to New Zealand this summer to live in Narnia!" They couldn't have been happier or prouder of their old man.

Work began that very week at KNB, which is located in Van Nuys, California. My two best friends and I started KNB in 1988 (Robert Kurtzman = K, Greg Nicotero = N, and Howard Berger = B). We had been comrades in arms for years before we began KNB, but we always knew we wanted to start our own shop some day and

rule the universe. We started out in an 800-square-foot space and we now inhabit a 22,000-square-foot shop that houses all the creatures, animals, and now Narnians that we've brought to life these past eighteen years.

The world of Narnia is divided into good guys and bad guys—a whole host of Fauns, Red Dwarfs, Gryphons, Satyrs, Unicorns, Minotaurs, Black Dwarfs, Boggles, Wolves, and many others.

The first step toward bringing these Narnians to life was to think about who they are and what they did prior to the battle. They needed to have backstories that would help us understand them better. For example, we have these little guys called Boggles. They are referenced in the book and Weta had designed them to be small molelike creatures. I liked the design, but wanted to make more sense of them. I felt that on the battlefield they would be crushed right out of the gate by a Centaur riding over them, so we brainstormed and I went to Andrew and said I feel that Boggles are underground dwellers that harvest vegetation.

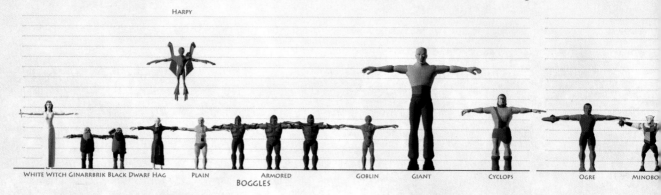

HARPY

WHITE WITCH   GINARRBRIK   BLACK DWARF   HAG   PLAIN   ARMORED   GOBLIN   GIANT   CYCLOPS   OGRE   MINOBO
                                             BOGGLES

RILLA | RUMBLEBUFFIN BADGER SQUIRRELS MRS. MR. RED DWARF FOREST CHERRY BLOSSOM NAIAD SATYR FAUN MR. TUMNUS FATHER XMAS LUCY EDMUND SUSAN PETER MER PEOPLE
GIANT | BEAVER FAMILY | DRYADS | PEVENSIES

They rarely come up top but have been suckered into joining the White Witch in her efforts to battle Aslan and his army. They would gladly go back underground and be left alone. We thought about what they might be related to and we came up with a hairless mole as our point of reference in redesigning to make them feel real. They were very wrinkled, had piggish snouts, sloth-like hands and feet for digging and wore almost nothing but a little loin cloth. Once Andrew agreed with this concept I spoke to Richard and he devised a wonderful weapon for them, a combination hoe and hatchet tool that made perfect sense; form follows function. This is the type of life we wanted to breathe into our children of Narnia. We felt if we believed in them, then everyone would.

Let me explain the first step to breathing life into a creature. Once you have a successful design, you have

your sculptors begin visualizing them in clay, sculpting three-dimensional versions of what you want them to resemble. I was very lucky to have one of the greatest sculptors in our business on this show, Mitch DeVane. I looked toward Mitch to help revise Weta's design for the Cyclops and make more sense of it in the practical world.

Once a sculpture is completed, it's sent to the moldmaking department. On this show my mold-shop supervisor was Jim Leonard. Jim and his crew make the molds out of syntactic dough, a strong yet lightweight material used on the space shuttle panels. Then they make a core by pressing a three-quarter-inch layer of clay into the open halves of the negative mold. After the molds are reassembled, they're left to harden until the next day.

The next stop is the foam department. Ben Rittenhouse is our foam

TOP: *Diagram of Aslan's army.*

OPPOSITE CENTER: *A Boggle.*

ABOVE: *A Gorilla.*

BELOW: *Diagram of the White Witch's army.*

NEXT PAGES: *Hags at the White Witch's camp.*

RAVEN

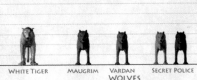

WARRIORS WEREWOLF SATYR ANKLESLICER POLAR BEAR WHITE TIGER MAUGRIM VARDAN SECRET POLICE
MINOTAURS | | | | | | | WOLVES

supervisor, and he and Monster Makers devised a
new system just for this film. The requirement I
gave Ben was that the foam needed to be as light
and fluffy as fresh cheesecake, but durable enough
to withstand the torture each skin would endure.
Ben and his crew pour the foam into a large foam-
injection gun and shoot it into the mold, filling
the narrow gap between syntactic dough and clay.
The mold is then placed into a huge oven and
baked for six hours. When the cooled mold is
opened, it reveals a perfect skin made of Ben's
special foam rubber.

From that stage the baked skins go to the
seaming and patching department to have the
thin seams trimmed and burned away with a
seaming iron. The seamers then foam-patch the
skins, filling any little imperfections, and rebake
the skins to cure the newly added foam patches.

Next stop, the painting room, where talented
artists such as Scott Patton paint the skins to look
like real flesh. The artists apply what we call RCP,
rubber cement paints, mixed with tints. Using a
combination of airbrushing and hand painting,
they add each freckle, capillary, vein, and pimple.

Even a sunburn was added to the Cyclops to make them feel that they are not really outdoor sort of guys, but this war had forced them out without sunblock and they got kissed by the sun.

In the back of the shop is the mechanical department run by David Wogh. Here the boys figure out how to bring the facial movements and articulation to life. I always stress that things need to look as organic as possible. We are so used to seeing how our faces move and we need to recreate these subtle twitches and expressions in the mechanical heads we're creating. Everything about each Narnian is very specific. Obviously, a Cyclops has only one eye, and so we designed the color and look of each eyeball and made them again using molds and cores. They are all acrylic, hand painted painstakingly and then cast and polished to look real. The mechies, as we call them, then design their interworkings for each creature. Almost like building bone, muscle, arteries, and a brain, but instead of organic material, we use vacuform plastic for skulls, cables for muscle, and radio control signals for the brain. It takes a long time to complete a head from beginning to end, and when it comes time to see it all come to life, it is magical. I always love to see the first test of the creature move because it's kind of like a Frankenstein factor: we are bringing it to life.

The finishing touches on the heads are final paint detailing, eye lashes, hair punched into the skin one at a time (another consuming aspect), and then we test it all on an actor and see how it comes to life. With each Narnian we created, Andrew was there to see it in all its glory. He would look at it, walk around it, study it—with a furrowed brow most of the time. He would then make his comments and suggestions and then finish up the meeting with the patented Andrew quote: *"This looks very promising. We are on the right track and good job."* Then I knew he liked it.

When I think about the hardest character to bring to life for this film, it has to be Mr. Tumnus. Andrew stated early on how important Tumnus was to him. He had a very specific idea of who and what he was since he first read the books as a child. The first step in creating Tumnus was to find the right actor to fill the bill. Weta had created a "fauntastic" sculpture study that said it all. I felt this was my favorite maquette they produced. After a long search led by our English casting director Gail Stevens and many actors later, Andrew came to me and said, "I think I found our Mr. Tumnus, but he is not available and we will have to work around his schedule." We needed as much time as possible to create all the pieces of Mr. Tumnus and at first I argued with Andrew that we needed an actor who was accessible to us, or I could not guarantee how he would end up. Andrew asked me to think about it and see if I could figure something out. I looked into his eyes and realized that if he did not get this actor, then it would not be the Tumnus from his childhood. How could I do that to Andrew? "Yes, Andrew, hire James McAvoy and I will make it work."

ABOVE: *Tumnus maquette.*

BELOW: *James tries on Tumnus's ears and horns.*

That week James was on a plane, sneaking out of England where he was filming a TV show. On Friday night after they wrapped, he traveled to L.A. arriving late Saturday afternoon, where he was picked up, brought to CyberFX to be cyber-scanned so we could have his full body proportions, then brought to KNB for life casting and test fittings. James had only six hours in L.A. and then he would have to board a plane again.

letter to Andrew thanking him for forcing me to make this work as James was Tumnus and no one else could ever be. I felt that aside from being a great actor, he would soon become a very good friend during the shoot and after.

In thinking about which is my favorite bad guy, I would have to say General Otmin the Minotaur. Within him, I was able to finally make a character that encompassed two big influences, a

At this time, we had just cyber-scanned a full-size Aslan figure based on Weta's maquette for him. It stood full size in the shop ready for molding. James walked in, looked around with his very tired but excited eyes, and spotted the figure of Aslan. He dropped his knapsack, slowly walked over to the sculpture, knelt down on one knee, bowed his head and said, "My Lord, Aslan."

Yes this was our Mr. Tumnus, 1,000 percent. After the life-cast session, and saying our good-byes to Mr. McAvoy, I sat down and wrote a long

mountain gorilla and one of my favorite children's book characters.

I knew Otmin had to be great and powerful—after all, he was the White Witch's general. Luckily Weta Workshop had designed a beautiful maquette for the Minotaur. They combined the head of a bull with that of a little buffalo (another one of my favorite creatures on earth), a man's body, and the legs of a bull with huge hooves. I knew that first we needed to find the right actor to play it. A lot of times productions make the mistake of hiring large muscle-bound stuntmen to play creatures, but the best are stuntmen/actors/performers that are tall, but not too huge. The suit will create the mass, not the actor. The person inside needs to have as much mobility as possible so that he can perform the feats required.

Since the wear and tear on the full-body sculpture would be great (a point proven with the Boggle suits), I wanted it all fabricated, meaning that each muscle was to be created from different densities of mattress foam to build pecs, traps, calves, you name it. I wanted the bone to be

strong and durable so that the skin would writhe over it, and so we sculpted rib cages and knees and shins and spines, ran them in a high-density foam, and then had them sewn in the proper places to make it all work. Think of it as if you are building a real creature: we start with the skeleton, then the muscle, then the veins (which were lengths of tygon tubing sewn to the muscle groups where needed like in the foams), and so forth. Then the skin is added. I chose a color I liked for the Minotaurs' skin, which was a kind of blueberry stain. Beth Hathaway, the head of our fabrications department, and her team patterned it

all out and created a full skin out of this dyed, 3-D, four-way stretch spandex skin that would cover the foam bone and muscle. It looked great!

Andrew came to see a demonstration of the suit to start getting his head wrapped around what could be accomplished on set. We dressed an actor, Derek Mears, in the prototype suit and he performed wonderfully (actor Shane Rangi eventually played Otmin). Andrew liked it but wanted to see more movement beneath the skin. We discussed using water-filled sacks in the chests to give that jiggle, but how could we show compressing bicep muscles?

One day I was thinking about using a technique we had for abs, which are sewn pockets filled with small plastic beads that gave us movement but also gave us the hard belly we were looking for. I suggested to Beth that we sew some larger pockets in the shape of a bicep muscle, really pack it tight with those beads and voilà, it worked. When the actor would flex, the muscle grew in size as a real one does. This was very cool and very simple. Once we made the modifications, Andrew came back in and we had Derek run around with his jiggling chest, flexing his biceps. Andrew loved it.

The next step was the hardest. We had to tie all the hair into the spandex skin one at a time. Mark Bolie, who ran the hair department, gathered a slew of talented ventilators to do this. For the next four months, they would all sit in these rooms tying away day and night to make the deadline, one hair at a time. It is amazingly painstaking, but the end result is unlike anything else. As part of our build, we did Otmin and twenty-four other Minotaurs. This was on top of all the other characters that required the same treatment, such as the Minoboars, the Satyrs, and, of course, Mr. Tumnus.

The Minotaur would be the first mechanical head the boys had to come up with. Because we had so many to make, twenty-five of them, Dave

Wogh, the head of the mechanical department, came up with a way to mass reproduce the parts with his small team made up of Jeff Edwards and Rob Derry. They felt if all the parts were made the same with no difference in fabrication, they could all go together like a model kit. Once the sculpture was completed by Scott Patton, it was molded, then cored, and the core mold was handed over to the mechies so they could create a vacuform shell to produce the skulls to mount all the mechanisms to. Then Jeff used a machine to design and mill all the tiny parts that went into making eye, jaw, lip, snarl, nose snort, blinks, and more movements required for each head. They assembled it all over the five-month prep, designing it all to operate and be puppeteered on set utilizing radio controls. Once we worked out the bugs and finessed everything, these guys were alive—moving, talking, growling, and even able to sing any Billy Idol song perfectly.

June came up on us fast and it was time to start to pack what was done and head off to New Zealand. I was leaving behind a lot of stuff to be finished, but I trusted my partner Greg Nicotero and the team and received updates daily. I first went by myself to set up and hire a local crew. I flew into Auckland on June 6, 2004, and began work immediately.

Prior to leaving I contacted a brilliant makeup artist and good friend, Tami Lane, to see if she was available to work with me on this show. Tami had started at KNB almost ten years prior when she came in with a tour group from Bradley University. Out of everyone, she made the biggest impression on me as she had made business cards on a paddleball toy. Aside from liking playing with it, I always had Tami's name in front of me as I paddled away. Once Tami graduated, she made the move to L.A. and we hired her to work in the shop. No matter what job we gave her, she always batted 100 percent. When *The Lord of the Rings* was crewing up, Richard Taylor called me and stated that he had received over 5,000 resumes and CVs and was not sure who to hire. I recommended three

ABOVE: *Tami airbrushes subtle colors onto James's nose.*

BELOW: *Sarah applies Satyr makeup.*

people, and one of them was Tami, although she did not send her resume to him.

That night Richard called Tami and offered her the job. The next morning Tami came in a little shell-shocked and asked me what I thought. I stated that she should take this job as it is a once-in-a-lifetime chance. She was concerned that if she left for the next four years, she might not be welcome back at KNB. I assured her she would and if she did not take the job she was fired. That weekend Tami left for New Zealand.

So Tami was on board for Narnia and I could not be happier. Aside from having one of the best makeup artists in New Zealand, I also had my old friend back for the next seven months. I wanted her to head the department, especially after *The Lord of the Rings*, where she handled Gimli's day-to-day application on top of tons of Orcs and Uruk-hai. Aside from running all the set work with me, Tami assembled the massive crew, all forty-two of them, and handled the final design and application of Mr. Tumnus, Ginarrbrik, about ten other Fauns, Dwarfs, and anyone else that had been standing there without

Satyr looks. The other Kiwi makeup artists and suit handlers we brought on board were Abby Vickery, Maryanne Rushton, Jess Reedy, Liz Blackwell, Laurelle Ziento, Shannon Mclean, Ray Massa, Tanya Bermingham, Haley Oliver, Linda Hal Couper, Annamarie Connors, and Tammy Green.

Once we had gobbled up all we could find in New Zealand, we went to Australia and landed everyone who had just finished on *Star Wars: Episode III.* They were so skilled, I could give any of them a character and they would run with it and make them great. Katharine Brown handled the building of all three female Boggles and Oreius, Aslan's Centaur General, who was played by Patrick Kake. Bliss Macgillicuddy started with us applying makeup and then ended up supervising, designing, and maintaining all the hairstyles each character wore, along with her talented crew Dalia Fernandez, Pip Lund, and Paige Banenoch. We also nabbed Paul Katte, Elka Wardega, Kerrin Jackson, Ado Atwood, Kristelle

their makeup applied to them. On this show Tami was my teacher as well as my muse.

I was limited to nine people I could bring from my crew in the States: Beth Hathaway, Dawn Dinninger, Sarah Rubano, Harrison "Little Al" Lozanzana, Dave Wogh, Rob Derry, Fred Fraliegh, Jeff Himmel, and Clare Mulroy—someone from every department.

We set up four makeup trailers and these amazingly huge circus tents at each location. Peta Sinclair was responsible for these fortresses of creatures and they were the best I had ever been in and used—dressing rooms, wood floors, heaters, air conditioning, makeup stations, running hot and cold water, microwave ovens, everything we needed. I keep photos of these structures with me when I go on job interviews to say, "Hey, this is how to do it and nothing else will be as good, so do it this way, the Kiwi way."

We then began to hire the makeup artists and suit dressers we needed to pull this off. Sean Foot had worked with me back on *Hercules* and *Xena* and is as talented as Tami—plus, he has a dry sense of humor. Sean took over the Centaur and

ABOVE: *Bliss works in some last curls to Oreius's hairstyle.*

RIGHT: *Sean transforms Allison Sarofim into a Centaur.*

Gardiner, and Sonny Tilders, who was the final ingredient to the mechie department with Dave and Robbie. Those guys were all meant to be together.

We had one Irish and a few American stragglers we found from other departments or they just came to visit us while we were there and they stayed for the run of the show. There was Lenny MacDonald, Mark Bourque, Jeanne Voslo, Mark Ballou, Patrick Mullan, and Roxie Hodenfield, who happened to be married to our first assistant director, K. C. Hodenfield, so I grabbed her up to join the army; plus we had worked with her on several of Robert Rodriquez's films in Texas and we already loved her.

The last country we invaded was Canada and I was able to bring over Sarah Graham and Rebeccah Delchambre, both very talented artists I had worked with before in their neck of the woods and I knew I could rely on them and they would be the final pieces of this puzzle.

I had my team of experts and we were all ready to face the hardest job of our lives, but also the most rewarding. The next seven months would be a whirlwind experience that would bring us all closer than strangers from all over the globe could hope to be. We would laugh, cry, be happy, get angry, you name it, but at the end of the show, we were family forever. This is something most people will never know or experience, especially on a film set, but it is all true. I fell in love with each person on the show and feel I have made a lot of new friends for life. Why, I am indeed the richest man in town, George Bailey!

I could go on and on for hundreds of more pages, but the publisher would not like that. I hope you enjoy the rest of the adventure into Narnia as much as I did and still do.

BELOW: *The last shots with these creatures on the last day of filming at the battlefield.*

NEXT PAGES: *Conceptual painting of the scene at the Stone Table.*

THREE'S COMPANY: THE MINOTAUR, THE DWARF, AND THE CENTAUR

FILMMAKING MAKES STRANGE bedfellows, and even stranger housemates. Only on this movie could you find a house with Otmin, the Minotaur General of the White Witch's Army; Ginarrbrik, a Dwarf and special assistant to the White Witch; and Oreius, the Centaur General of Aslan's forces—also known respectively as actors Shane Rangi, Kiran Shah, and Patrick Kake.

Because their makeup process was so intense, their battle scenes so involved, and the training so demanding, we found that these three needed to be as close to the set as possible. But one has limited options when shooting on top of a mountain. So when we found a tiny alpine village near the mountain, we created one of the most dynamic households ever assembled.

"We all looked after the house and kept it clean," says actor Kiran Shah (Ginarrbrik). "We got on really well with each other. After work Patrick would generally do the cooking, as he loved to do. When I got home Patrick and Shane would usually be playing guitar; Shane would teach me a new chord. They were also into heavy fitness routines for their parts, and so they showed me new ways to train. I had to learn to use the whip and how to crack it. And stunt coordinator Allan Poppleton put me through intensive training to fight with an axe."

Patrick Kake (General Oreius) took the longest in makeup. As the leader of Aslan's army, he had to look amazing. Andrew wanted this movie to be the definitive source for movie Centaurs. Patrick was up at 3:00 A.M. every morning, then three hours for the prosthetic facial makeup, then another hour for flocking—the process by which the makeup artists applied the Centaur hair to the body. In this case, they used a static gun with the tiny hairs and glue inside to shoot the hair on the body. Then they used an airbrush to touch it up, give it that natural Centaur look. Add another two hours at the end of each long day just to take it all off.

With all those extreme battle sequences, injuries could also be a problem. Actor Shane Rangi (General Otmin) was no stranger to pain. He'd lost an eye on the rugby field and lost some of his teeth during a stunt when a horse galloped over him on the set of another picture. In order to play the White Witch's main Minotaur, Shane had to wear an extensively designed animatronic bull's head, which rendered him essentially blind. You find out pretty quickly just how good an actor someone is when they have to hit their marks without being able to see anything. Shane proved to be brilliant.

Sometimes they'd pass out from exhaustion, sometimes they'd go next door for a bonfire party thrown by their neighbor, the White Witch, Tilda Swinton.

They did manage to enjoy themselves in the battle, too. Shane's favorite scene as Otmin was taking out two Centaurs in the battle. Patrick's favorite scene in the battle was taking out his housemate, Shane: "I just hammer him. Double sword to the back."

They came home one night and looked at the call sheet for the next day. "Oh, Shane, tomorrow, what have we got here? Hmmm, oh look! Otmin buys the farm! Sorry, Shane." But even after a long day of slaughter on the battlefield, Patrick roasted the chicken for his flatmates that night for dinner.

OPPOSITE: *Kiran Shah (Ginarrbrik) is the White Witch's assistant.*

TOP RIGHT: *Shane Rangi (Otmin) is the Minotaur General.*

BOTTOM RIGHT: *Patrick Kake as Oreius.*

REAL MAGIC: CREATING THE SPECIAL EFFECTS OF NARNIA

By Dean Wright, Supervisor of Visual Effects

MY ADVENTURES MAKING *THE LION,*
the Witch and the Wardrobe (LWW) began in the
neighboring land of Middle Earth. As the visual
effects producer for Peter Jackson's *The Lord of the*
Rings trilogy, I was in Queenstown, New Zealand,
for a few days with Barrie Osborne, the producer
of the *Rings* films, and Jim Rygiel, the trilogy's
visual effects supervisor, shooting some last-
minute scenic footage along a New Zealand South
Island river, which was needed for a scene in *The*
Return of the King. Barrie, it turns out, was a long-
time friend of Mark Johnson, the producer for *The*
Lion, the Witch and the Wardrobe, who by chance was
also in Queenstown for the day, scouting various
New Zealand locations with Andrew Adamson,
the director of the film, for their upcoming Narnia
picture. That evening, Barrie, Jim, and I met with
Mark and Andrew for a fantastic dinner together
as the two major productions merged for an
evening and swapped stories. We chatted about
our experiences on *Rings,* while Andrew told
us what his vision for Narnia was, and
together we discussed ways one might
carry off the enormous challenges the
film would present.

Months later, instead of packing up for home, I was preparing to move from Wellington to Auckland and step up into the role as the visual effects supervisor for Narnia.

What separates this film from all others is the sheer number of lead and supporting characters that are either entirely digital (or CG—computer graphics) creations or are enhanced in some way digitally (Tumnus's legs, for example). Aslan, the Beavers, the Fox, Maugrim, and Vardan are all CG characters, and all of the Fauns, Satyrs, Minotaurs, and Minoboars have reverse legs (like a goat's) that needed to be attached and animated digitally to the actors many months after shooting was done.

For each of the hundreds and hundreds of visual effects shots, a plan of action (or methodology) needed to be created on how to achieve the effect Andrew desired. That was my job as visual effects supervisor: make a plan, keep a budget, coordinate hundreds of workers, and make it happen. For instance, in the early preproduction period, we had chosen as our main visual effects vendor, Rhythm & Hues (R&H). But we soon discovered that the number of visual effects needed and their costs were both growing. Our solution, after many meetings and phone calls, was to award about half the work to another visual effects vendor. Sony Pictures Imageworks (SPI) and Industrial Light and Magic (ILM) were both anxious to be considered. We chose SPI based on the strength of their animation work to date, but

OPPOSITE: *The coronation scene, pre-effects.*

ABOVE: *Anna with Dean Wright.*

would ultimately come back to ILM as well (more on that later). By making aggressive deals with both R&H and SPI for their respective work, we were able to bring our budget back in line.

Our visual effects production team, led by Randy Starr, our visual effects producer, and Libby Hazell, our visual effects coproducer, broke down each shot and generated the list of items (or elements) needed for each sequence so they could be studied and integrated into the shooting schedule by K. C. Hodenfield, our assistant director.

Of course the competing demands of the weather concerns (it changes constantly), the shortened length of the shooting day due to the actors' ages, and the practicalities of what scenes could be photographed on location or had to be shot onstage, in addition to the visual effects requirements, would all be considered as we formulated the plan of attack.

Take, as an example, the scene where Peter, Susan, and Lucy first meet Aslan. In the camp, there are meant to be several thousand troops preparing for the final battle with the evil White Witch. In reality we had fewer than a hundred of the "good" creatures on location; visual effects would fill out the ranks. Our first step is to break down the shot into separate pieces. We had to decide what could be shot in the original photography on set (called the "hero plate"), and what would be added later, either as a separate photographic element (either as a second "plate" pass, a "green-screen element," etc.), or a digital character or element. For the Aslan camp scenes, we wanted to shoot the kids in the hero plates, along with as many actors in prosthetics as we could have ready and available when the kids were ready to go.

We would need to add the CG legs to all of the Fauns and Satyrs, the bottom section to the Centaurs (half human-half horse), and all of the other creatures that live only in the computer, including Leopards, Cheetahs, Badgers, Boars, Gorillas, Bears, and of course the Beavers and Aslan!

We decided the best way for the reverse leg creatures to be photographed was to have them wear green tights and place reflective reference markers on them. This would allow us to use "on-set motion capture" to record their movements whenever possible, or at least provide a visual reference for the animators to use to guide their leg animation.

For any of the shots with green-legged creatures, we would also need a separate empty version of the shot (called a "clean plate"). A clean plate allows us to paint back in the parts of the set or location that are covered up in the hero plate

with unwanted items but need to be seen in the final version of the shot. Since the digital creatures' legs would be different shapes than the actors' green-tights legs, there were sections behind them that would be obscured in the hero plate, but would be revealed when the animated legs were added later. Also, all of the Centaur's legs would require a height adjustment, and platforms would be required and photographed in the hero plates, but would need to be replaced with the grass, rocks, and other set items that live underneath or behind them.

Additionally, if the shot called out for one of our hero CG characters (Aslan, Beavers, etc.), a size and lighting reference pass would need to be shot with life-size, handcrafted, stuffed and computer-laser-cut polystyrene animal replicas, which we referred to collectively as "stuffies." These stuffies would also prove to be a great tool for the camera department for shot lineup, as many of the shots either started from or traveled with the CG characters, and this would provide a stand-in for the camera operators to frame with and the camera assistants to focus to. If the CG characters moved within the shot, I would walk the path, with the

stuffies, that Andrew directed them to travel and have this path photographed, so not only would we have a great reference for how the characters would look in the various lighting situations within a given location or set, we would have a record of what Andrew wanted the characters to do, which would provide the editors and eventually the animators with a guide to follow. We would also shoot a silver ball (for lighting reference) and a gray ball (for light/dark contrast reference) to aid in matching the on-set lighting when creating and lighting the CG characters later in the computer.

Since the size of the camp and the number of creatures was only a fraction of the amount we would want to see eventually on-screen, we needed to extend digitally the set and creatures beyond what was built and dressed on location. This would mean adding more tents, weapons, forges, etc., along with thousands of Aslan's troops. For the added troop numbers, many of

OPPOSITE: *Susan and Lucy with Tumnus and soldiers in green tights.*

ABOVE: *Centaur's height adjustment.*

NEXT PAGES: *Adding more tents to expand the camp.*

the shots would require some sophisticated crowd simulations while others could be populated with a library of green screen elements, which we would shoot after the hero plates were photographed. For several shots, we would need to see far beyond the camp area, all the way out to the sea where the castle of Cair Paravel sits. This would require us to shoot a separate environment with cliffs and sea from a helicopter that could then be added to the hero plates.

This process was repeated for every shot in the film and all of the information organized into a manageable list (or database) for dissemination to all of the other picture departments.

BRINGING THE CHARACTERS TO LIFE

Besides the four Pevensie kids, the White Witch, and the Professor, a number of key roles would be realized almost exclusively as computer created characters. The six key digital characters were Aslan (the Lion), Mr. and Mrs. Beaver, the Fox, and Maugrim and Vardan (the head Wolves of the White Witch's police). Many other digital characters were required to help fill out the camp and battle scenes, but these six characters had to act and deliver a performance as entertaining and emotionally moving as the actors we had on set for the film to work. Andrew also insisted that the characters had to look and move as realistically as the actors on set.

Aslan Creating
Aslan was complicated in many ways. Aslan would be called upon to deliver many dramatic moments in the film, and so we needed to create a photo-realistic CG Lion that could stand up to the scrutiny of any potential camera angle. Then we would have to build animation controls into him that would allow the computer artists to give him a range of expressions and emotions beyond that of a real lion, but still within the level of audience acceptability for what a lion could do.

A host of reference material was either shot or acquired to decide exactly what this creature should look like. Andrew chose specific features from the various reference photos and footage to use as the basis for Aslan and then guided the development process at R&H for over a year to create a character that was ready for a close-up.

During this development process, the actual skeleton of the Lion was built, along with the proper muscles, skin, eyes, teeth, etc. Achieving the final look, however, would require our visual effects company to write more sophisticated software that allowed the digital Lion's fur and mane to look and move exactly like those of a real lion.

Once the model was created, a number of animation tests were carried out to ensure that his movements and facial expressions met with Andrew's expectations.

While most of Aslan's moments on screen would be filled with the digital character, a physical animatronic Lion would also be needed for several scenes where characters physically handled him. Howard Berger's team at KNB worked hand in hand with R&H to create several versions of the Lion that would match the CG Lion exactly in features, look, and size for these moments.

Howard also created a puppet head for us to use on set for camera framing and lighting reference. I also occasionally donned a BMX vest outfitted with a speed rail connection so I could move around the set wearing the Aslan head to aid the kids when blocking out and shooting some of the scenes.

Our original plan was to use one of the KNB Lions for on-set camera framing. The time and crew needed to handle the creatures was more than we could dedicate given the tight shooting schedule we faced. Before too long we realized that we would need to create a more portable full-size replica of our Lion. We took the computer model created by R&H and gave it to our art department. They in turn used a computer-controlled laser cutter to sculpt a life-size Aslan out of polystyrene, painted him, and rolled him on set. We used our new Styro-Aslan extensively for the rest of the shoot, and even threw an Aslan hairpiece on him so we could get our lighting and size reference in the same footage. Despite being much lighter and easier to move around than the animatronic Lions, our Styro-Aslan still required at least two people to carry him on and off the set, and we actually had to airlift him via helicopter to the mountain location for the final fight between Peter and the White Witch. The crew stopped to watch as Aslan flew in overhead.

Mr. and Mrs. Beaver

The Beavers have a crucial role in the film. Mr. Beaver is the first animal the Pevensies meet in Narnia, and we needed the character to make a transition from a realistic beaver to a talking, acting creature to help the kids as well as the audience accept the premise that all of the animals in Narnia are capable of this as well.

In more practical terms, the Beavers were also the first fully digital characters the actors would be scheduled to "work with."

The KNB team made us two life-size Beaver stuffies based on artwork and sculptures designed by the Weta Art Department under Andrew's direction. We used the Beaver stuffies for every one of their scenes, not only for camera framing and lighting reference, but also for the kids to act against.

Again, CG models were built by digital artists and presented to Andrew at various stages of development for approval. The key story point the Beavers had to deliver was their relationship with the kids. The humor they brought to the film necessitated them to become a bit more anthropomorphic than any of the other animal-based creatures in Narnia. As such, they needed to

OPPOSITE: *Andrew with Anna and Georgie.*

ABOVE: *Transporting Aslan's head.*

BELOW: *Mr. and Mrs. Beaver stuffies.*

189

have a wide capability for expressions and emotions and would also need to be able to walk on either two or four legs, depending on the scene. Switching between the two modes in a realistic manner was challenging. Making the fur photo-realistic in the wide varieties of lighting situations also proved to be very demanding, as again the charge from Andrew was that the Beavers should look and move like real creatures, albeit slightly more humanized.

The Fox The character of the Fox has a small but pivotal role in the film. He single-handedly saves the Pevensies and the Beavers from the White Witch's Wolf goon squad, then bravely stands up to the Witch in spite of the risk he's placed himself in. His actions are key to Edmund's realization of how he must act later when placed in a similar situation.

Andrew wanted to base the Fox on a very realistic fox, and so the Imageworks team was given some photos of a real fox to use as a guide in creating the CG version. The character's performance would need to present a charming-but-tough, cute-but-serious persona to pull off the moments Andrew wanted. This required us to not only have another actor on set to read the lines of dialogue, but months of interaction with the animation supervisor and technical leads to get the right looks and attitude for the scene.

ABOVE AND OPPOSITE: *Pre-viz and final scene of Peter leading the charge into battle.*

NEXT PAGES: *Peter, Susan, and Lucy at Aslan's camp.*

The Battle When Peter leads Aslan's troops into battle against the forces of the White Witch, he is taking an army of roughly 5,000 Centaurs, Fauns, Satyrs, Leopards, Cheetahs, and the like straight into an army numbering 15,000. In actuality, when shooting these scenes at Flock Hill, which is an hour or so outside of Christchurch, we had about 150 actors, stuntmen, and extras total to play both sides. The remaining army was to be filled in with digital creatures.

In order to figure out exactly what would be needed for each and every shot, we would turn to an incredibly useful resource—the previsualizations (or animatics—kind of like mini-animated movies) created for the film by our own team of animators led by pre-viz supervisor Rpin Suwannath.

The previsualization of the main sequences in the film had begun long before I was brought on board and continued even after shooting had finished. Andrew would take the fully animated shots and cut them together with Sim Evan-Jones and Jim May, our editors, into complete sequences covering the major action beats of nearly every scene in the film that would require some kind of visual effect. The rest of the film was filled in with storyboards. In the end, we had a complete version of the film cut together before we ever rolled any film. We used the animatics extensively during the planning stages of the movie, continually refining them until Andrew was satisfied and then dissecting them for the details required to plan out the shooting needs.

During filming, we would usually start our shooting day by reviewing the relevant pre-viz with the department heads and camera operators and Andrew and Don would decide which parts to follow and which to use as a rough guide for the day's shooting. While this was a valuable planning guide for many scenes, it would prove to be an essential tool used throughout the battle sequences, especially those directed by Phil Neilson, our stunt coordinator and second unit director.

Ultimately, the solution for this monumental task was similar to others we would use on the film, a collection of digital solutions to enhance the original photography. We would shoot the scenes with as many creatures we could make up, armor up, and deliver up to the set. We would place the real characters close to camera, with the next layer of creatures to be key-frame animated, and the background filled with characters created with the latest version of Massive, the crowd and battle simulation software first developed for *The Lord of the Rings* trilogy, but revised and enhanced to accommodate the increased types and varieties of creatures that would end up battling one another in the climactic scenes of our film.

For shots where the foreground action was meant to feature a CG-only character (like a Leopard, Werewolf, or even a Centaur charging at full gallop), the camera team would use the extensive previsualizations as a guide to what the CG characters would be doing and how they would move. The mid-grounds then would be filled with real creatures, with space allowed in between for added key-frame animated characters, and the background filled again with Massive armies.

LIVING WITH ENHANCEMENTS

Because of the differences in physical anatomy, you can't sit, move, or walk like a human and expect to look like a Faun or Satyr.

The key Faun in the film and the first character you meet in Narnia is Mr. Tumnus, who was played by the amazingly talented James McAvoy. James had arrived in New Zealand just days before he was to start shooting and had limited time with Andrew prior to arriving. One of the first issues we needed to address was how James should physically stand, move, and walk on set so that when the digital legs are added later, his stance, balance, and movements look natural and integrated into his body. As James would be not only the first but also the most important Faun in the film, whatever we decided would be the basis for all of the on-set Fauns and Satyrs to follow.

To solve this, we built a little motion-capture stage next to one of our studio stages and ran through a series of tests with James to help determine what the movement limitations were and lock down exactly what type of human walk translated best to a Faun. James reading his lines, and me on my knees reading the role of Lucy, provided not only great humor for the crew but also a chance for James to explore his character's movements, which would also provide a base for his character's personality. We tried various types of foot positions, believing that James would likely need to stand on his tiptoes for most of the scenes.

In between camera set-ups, Andrew would come by and see the result of our testing along-side the actual movements James was trying. Seeing the real-time results of these tests proved invaluable, as James and Andrew were able to see immediately what worked and what didn't, and we quickly got a foot-and-leg action that translated best to a Faun and was also easier to perform throughout a long shooting day.

This experimenting proved to be so valuable we extended this plan to define the motion for nearly all of our CG-augmented characters.

The character of Oreius, the Centaur most trusted by Aslan, also played by an actor on set, Patrick Kake, presented us with an entirely different challenge. Providing his lower horse-half was a critical issue to be solved, in that whatever methodology we chose to deploy for Oreius would also need to be implemented for every other Centaur (male and female) at Aslan's camp, the battle, and anywhere else they were seen.

One key challenge in photographing the Centaurs is the height difference that would exist between a human and a Centaur. When you add the upper human half to a horse in the proper Centaur scale relationship, the new creature stands about fifteen inches taller than the human alone. Since we wanted to shoot as many of the Centaurs as we could on location, we needed to solve this as efficiently as possible. We discussed the possibility of having the actors playing the Centaurs wear fifteen-inch raised stilt/boots, but since we were hiring local talent for these roles, and not members of Cirque du Soleil, we decided that adjustable and

ABOVE: *Translating James's movements into a Faun's.*

OPPOSITE: *Centaur General Oreius.*

portable platforms would be the best and safest solution for most of the shots. A Centaur couldn't move anywhere without a platform (or a series of them), which would be somewhat limiting, but it would suffice for the action required at Aslan's camp. (For the battle scenes when the Centaurs charge at full gallop, a total CG solution would be

couple of tests to confirm that our methodologies were sound. Within a few weeks, we were looking at a Centaur charge the camera—and it was very reassuring!

Additionally, the KNB team built a number of horse bodies that, when dressed in armor and attached to the Centaur actors, worked

the norm anyway.) We decided to use the Centaur's front armor plate as the blending point between the actor and CG creature. When we were adding a CG lower half, we would remove the Weta-designed live-action armor plate and add it back digitally, so it could move with the motion of the animated horse-half.

We shot several motion tests with some Centaur actors on film and had R&H produce a

splendidly for shots where the legs were not seen on camera. Because of the amount and type of muscle movement you would expect to see across the body when a Centaur walks, and the cumbersome rigging required for the horse-body attachments, however, the use of the horse bodies was sparse and could be used only for shots where the Centaurs did not move at all.

EYE TO EYE

Of course the main goal in filming is to shoot memorable performances. The actors provided them on a daily basis. But even the most experienced actor has trouble in a green-screen environment, reacting to places, things, or other characters that aren't there. Our film would be overflowing with these acting challenges, and our cast was mostly first-time actors. Our plan was to provide them with as much help on set as we could. This would include everything from having people on camera acting out the roles of the digital characters to placing stuffed Beavers, Foxes, Wolves, or Lions in the appropriate places, to having moving eye-line sticks for the kids to watch and follow (puppeteered by Andrew and me), for most of the scenes in the film. Ultimately, the kids would turn in performances that were more real, emotional, and connected to the digital characters than ever before captured on film.

For the first scene where the kids meet and talk to Mr. and Mrs. Beaver, Andrew decided to try to actually act out the scene with the kids on camera. Alina Phelan, Andrew's assistant (and a talented actress), and Andrew played the Beaver couple, and worked on the scene over and over with Will, Anna, Georgie, and Skandar, giving them the chance to interact with a performer, not just a tennis ball on a stick. This makes the hero plate digital-paint cleanup work more labor intensive, as we now have to replace quite a bit more background with unwanted people in the frame, but the one thing we can't change later is the actor's performance. It's either there or it's not, and if we have to do a little more work later in visual effects in order to get the performance Andrew is looking for on set, it is time and money well spent,

When the CG characters are moving around, though, a different technique is required to make sure the actors are looking at the proper eye lines for the CG characters. To accomplish this, we primarily used re-purposed carbon-fiber extendable boom poles. Boom poles are designed to be extended quite far in order for the sound department to keep their crew and equipment out of the camera frame. This would allow us to stand off camera and move character eye lines around the set for the kids yet still keep the frame fairly clean.

The first time we used the poles on set, I noticed that the kids were having difficulty adjusting to the very inexpressive tennis ball, and their eyes were drifting away from their mark. I thought there must be a better prop I could use. On the way home from set that evening, I stopped at the local grocery store (being the only store open that late at night) and went looking for some small stuffed animals I might be able to attach to the poles. In the back of the store, I found a bin filled with a collection of very small animal puppets. I bought the lot and the next morning, the kids, possessing great imaginations, found it much easier to focus on the little animals and it showed on film.

MINIATURES

Our use of miniatures in Narnia is limited, but essential. While there are several scenes in *LWW* that were shot on virtually 360 degrees of green screen, only one really required the use of physical miniatures to produce the final visual effects shots: the Frozen Waterfall sequence. The set for the Waterfall was actually only a slice of the Waterfall that Andrew ultimately wants to see in *LWW*. With the physical action that takes place in this scene, a combination of small- and large-scale miniature/water photography with advanced digital ice and water volumetric simulations would give this scene the dynamic impact it needs to propel the story forward.

The set itself was recreated in one-twelfth-scale miniature form and extended in both height and width. In shooting this set from various camera angles, we could take any of our set footage and push the far walls away to make the distance the kids need to travel much farther. This makes their position more precarious and dangerous. We would need to use a much larger scale model for the actual destruction for the ice cracking and water interactivity. A one-quarter-scale Waterfall would give us a good size shot at the proper frame rates, as long as everything mechanically works. The first take on events like these are rarely flawless, and this was no exception, as two-thirds of the model failed to move at all. The second take, however, was quite good, and the ice break and camera work worked together in concert.

OPPOSITE TOP: *Conceptual drawing for Mr. Beaver.*

OPPOSITE BOTTOM: *Using a stuffed Beaver, Andrew and Alina act out the scene with the kids.*

ABOVE: *Susan and Peter at the Frozen Waterfall.*

THE FINAL FRONTIER

The main portion of shooting finally came to an end in late December 2004, several hours before Christmas. After living in New Zealand for three years, I finally came home. Our holiday was too brief, and before long we were back at work planning our next phase, the cold winter shoot about to take place in the Czech Republic and Poland.

The weather had been our foil many times during our shooting schedule, with the rain, clouds, and sun appearing when least wanted, but we made it through it all. We were facing a new problem with the winter shoot, however. Our art department reported back to us some troubling news: it was the warmest winter in decades in Europe, and there wasn't any snow where we were planning to shoot. We pushed back the shoot several times, waiting for the cold snap to hit, but the news was not good. Finally, almost overnight, it all changed and the cold winds and snow came in with a fury.

Andrew turned to me and said, "You're going to the Czech Republic tomorrow to shoot the Gate!" The Gate is the name for an amazing Rock Bridge formation we would be using for a scene where the Beavers first show the kids the vast scope of Narnia. The opening shot for the scene would be a helicopter shot flying in toward and around the bridge showing off as much of the landscape as we could. The trick was we had already shot the green-screen portion of the shot—a big crane shot of the kids—and I had to shoot a helicopter background plate that would

Scouting snow in the Czech Republic.

hook up with this footage. There were several obstacles to getting the shot just right: first, we needed to be as low as possible, which meant flying in as close to the trees as possible; second, we needed to slow down as we came upon the bridge and rise up and around it, which is exactly the opposite thing a helicopter wants to do; and third, we needed to frame the bridge with as much space as possible in order to create the best-looking image, but a rock wall and the German border put some limits on that.

After several helicopter trips and multiple takes, we got several good ones for Andrew to choose from. Ideally, Andrew would have loved even more snow than we had, but, thanks to a little help from the computer, we enhanced what was there and made the whole scene look a little whiter.

Shortly thereafter, Andrew and the rest of the production team arrived and it became clear that I was to be given the task of directing the second unit. This would include everything from shots of the kids (doubles) running on a real frozen lake, shots of our cast in various snowy settings to background plates needed for a number of scenes in the film shot against green screens.

I don't believe we ever stayed in one place for more than a couple of days before we were sent to the next location that had just been dusted with fresh snow.

We journeyed across the Czech-Polish border several times, visited Krakow and Warsaw, in addition to Prague, as well as a host of smaller cities along the way. Our mission: keep moving higher up into the coldest areas with the most snow. We all felt a bit like a traveling band, hitting all the small venues across Poland and the Czech Republic, even unexpectedly walking across the border into Slovakia while scouting (it pays to always have your passport on you!).

We also had a still-photo team alongside us to take series of still images of any potential vistas or snowy mountains and forests, whenever they were spotted, to use as elements for background matte paintings.

POST-PRODUCTION

Finally, after all of the winter scenes were shot, all focus turned to the cutting room set up in an office building in downtown Hollywood. All along the way, we had been turning over filmed sequences to the visual effects companies to start the process of character and effects animation. For seven months we turned over everything that needed a creature, an arrow, or even a fly to a company to produce the work.

As I write this, we are now in the midst of this process. A portion of time is dedicated nearly every day for Andrew, me, and the editors to review the work in progress generated and presented by the facilities.

The animation work begins with a formal handover in the cutting room. We discuss the sequences and Andrew explains what he wants to happen in each of the shots. The facilities take the original camera negative and digitally scan it for use in the computer. The tracking team does their thing and hands the shot over to the animators.

The first time we review the work is usually when a very rough blocking pass has been completed. This would show the basic size, placement, and movement of the characters within the frame.

Once the blocking is approved, the animators would then refine the animation until Andrew was happy with the acting performance of the characters. The shot is then passed off for any secondary animation (eye blinks, muscle movements, etc.), furring or armoring (as

required), and lighting. Once this has all been approved, the composite of all the elements contained within the shot (characters, background, atmosphere, etc.) is completed and shot out on film for final review.

We now have a full team working alongside us to make sure the companies get the elements and data they need from us in a timely fashion, as well as track the iterations of the work and ensure the final shots are delivered once they have been approved. In addition to my role, I work with Randy Starr on our business side; Aaron Cowan, VFX production manager; Chris Anderson, VFX coordinator; Mark Simone and Andy Simonson, VFX production assistants— along with the editing team to whom we are attached at the hip.

Everyone on our team now, the editing team, the producers, the artists and support staff at R&H, SPI, and ILM, as well as those who have helped us along the way in virtually every department on the shoot, have all contributed to the creation of the effects in *The Lion, the Witch and the Wardrobe.*

It has been my honor to work alongside them, and my extreme pleasure to work side by side with Andrew to help bring this movie to the screen. I hope you enjoy watching it as much as we have enjoyed creating it for you.

Now I better get back to work to make sure all the shots are finished before you sit in the theater and watch Narnia become a real place to visit.

THE COSTUMES OF NARNIA: PUTTING THE WARDROBE INTO THE WARDROBE

THE COSTUMES OF *THE LION, THE WITCH and the Wardrobe* are the perfect fusion of art and epic-movie practicality. Tilda Swinton will tell you that for her, the character's wardrobe is the most important part of the role. As she sees it, the costume takes care of 90 percent of the part and she takes care of the other 10 percent.

"You get inspiration from everywhere," explains costume designer Isis Mussenden, who had to dress WWII soldiers and throngs of children in period dress, and clothe a menagerie of fantastic creatures and Skandar. Inspiration came to her from a Frozen Waterfall, a magazine photo, an avante garde artist, a museum, and a dead bird—and of course the book itself.

Such a vast array of costumes—both historical and fantastic—required meticulous research. The first thing Isis did was take a trip to London to visit the Museum of Childhood at the Victoria and Albert for historical research for the children in 1940s England.

"We were prepared to make an entire film in 1943 England," Isis says. "They had all the clothes in the archive. We had to research them because everything needed to be made." The clothes no longer existed, except as museum pieces. In fact, Isis's wardrobe crew made exact historical replicas of period clothing for the

---

OPPOSITE: *Edmund meets the White Witch.*

ABOVE: *Costume sketch by Hope Atherton.*

RIGHT: *Isis with White Witch sketches.*

Exact historical replicas of period clothing were made.

doesn't even exist anymore, so we had to find things that were close. Lucy's outfit from her Tumnus scenes, that little checkered dress with the smocking is one of my absolute favorites," she admits.

With a cast that included hundreds of extras, Isis had her hands full. Fortunately, besides being an extraordinarily talented designer, Isis is also a great manager. "I've got all these unbelievably talented people around me bringing me ideas. I like to open the door: if you inspire people, you get tenfold back. We'd get three or four people putting our heads together over a creative problem. Then it was my job to pull it all together and make it work."

Her stunning work with the White Witch is a wonderful example of that collaborative spirit. It started with an overall concept that Isis and Andrew came up with in the very beginning. Then Isis and Tilda sat down and thought through her character's wardrobe according to the story. Their first fittings with Tilda took six to seven hours on average because of the free exchange of ideas. "Tilda is amazing because she loves the process," Isis explains. "She inspired me. And she's the perfect canvas. She's got those long arms and torso and that face with its exquisite bone structure. She's a clear and gorgeous beauty. All strength from the inside."

When Isis originally asked Tilda to bring in some pictures that inspired her for the costumes so they could share their favorites, she was surprised by the results. Each of them showed up the next day with the exact same magazine photo of an Alexander McQueen dress.

One weekend when Tilda took a trip to the Huka Lodge in New Zealand, she returned with another idea: at Huka Falls she was taken with the simple, austere beauty of a Frozen Waterfall. From that, combined with Roger Ford's extensive ice images, the fabric was born. Isis took that idea one step further. She developed a fabric for one of the White Witch's dresses that resembled the

TOP: *Battle costumes.*

ABOVE: *Tilda and Isis at first fitting of the White Witch.*

OPPOSITE: *Hope Atherton's White Witch sketch.*

children in the first part of the movie, set during the London Blitz. "We had two women knitting every sweater, each pair of tights, the stockings for the girls, the socks for the boys with the old patterns on them, exactly the way we got samples from London so that they could copy them and we could find our own way. The yarn from that period

natural phenomenon: a fabric of fluid, frozen elegance. "We spent weeks trying different techniques," Isis says.

"Sarah Shepard, our fabulous textile artist from New Zealand, would show me things and I'd say, 'What if we did this?' And that really paid off when it came time to put it together. We put a different combination of things including a dyed piece of silk with felted wool and silk together on top of it. Then this lace we had hand-sewn and burnt out the back with organza pieces in ice shapes over it, and then it finally began to take flight. That ice was our concept because there were times you could look at this and you felt like you could put your hand right through it. The White Witch needed to be other-worldly," notes Isis. "She's half-giant, half-witch. She's not human and yet we have a human playing the part, but prosthetics wasn't the way to go. We played with that, but everything felt very alien." Another constraint was the corset. It kept Tilda's posture so erect that she couldn't sit down once the costume was on. To make matters worse, the combination of the White Witch's wig and crown was so heavy that we had to build a special "leaning board" so Tilda could give her body a rest between scenes.

The White Witch's crown is an artistic highlight of the film. To come up with something really special for the Queen of Narnia's crown, Isis collaborated with artist Hope Atherton, renowned in the art world for her fantastic, organic, and often breathtakingly macabre work.

"Hope really went to town with that crown," Isis says. "The very first time I read the book for the job I wanted an ice crown that melted and I can't believe that we got to do it. It was working with Hope that helped me sell the idea to Andrew.

"I always liked the idea of the ice crown, and as the White Witch's powers wane and the frozen winter thaws into spring, her crown gradually melts. That's when Hope came in; when we were talking about it, she was thrilled and then it went over to that world of hers. There were suddenly shards of ice shooting up and growing

ABOVE: *The White Witch in her ice crown.*

BELOW AND RIGHT: *Ice crown sketches.*

out of her head. The two of us work extremely well together, because I have ideas and practicality and she has that macabre brain of hers, that wonderful twist of the extraordinary no one else has."

Isis and Hope's collaboration also resulted in the sacrificial garment the White Witch dons for the show-stopping scene at the Stone Table. If you look closely at it, you'll see that the collar rising dramatically above the White Witch's neck is actually a taxidermied black rooster woven into the costume, a chilling flourish that reveals so much about the character's malevolence.

In another great touch, the White Witch wears Aslan's mane into the battle—a symbol of power for all her enemies to see. Isis explains, "It's as if she's telling these people, I'm your Queen and you've lost your king, and how irreverent I am to wear his fur."

To give Tilda the freedom of movement required for the battle scenes, the designers made her dress from ultralight titanium butcher chain from Germany. "Butchers' aprons are made out of small links of pure metal so the butchers don't cut themselves," Isis explains. "Well, this is stronger than that and even lighter in weight. We started with a lace dress, which seemed fussy and almost too pretty. It was much lighter but it didn't have the strength. Then we worked on it and refined it, and we made three of these battle skirts out of 3,200 links individually welded together into chainmail."

There were two major factors that allowed Isis the time to design something so exceptional for the White Witch in battle: Weta Workshop and Kimberly Adams. Weta handled the costumes for the battle—all the armor and weapons— except for the tunics, leaving Isis free for other

ABOVE: *The White Witch wears Aslan's mane.*

LEFT AND BELOW: *Hope's Stone Table costume sketches.*

207

costuming. "All the characters needed heraldry, the tunics and clothing underneath Weta's magnificent armor," Isis explains. "My associate designer, Kimberly Adams, was brilliant," says Isis. "I handed her the army and just said, 'Keep it going. We're going to do it together, but you've got to keep it going.' I mean, fifty-five costumes for just the Centaurs alone!"

For Isis the biggest puzzle of the movie was figuring out the difference between what would really show up on-screen and what would be added later with computer-generated imagery. "Having worked on a lot of CGI with Andrew as the costume designer on *Shrek* and *Shrek 2*, I had questions right off the bat. What's CGI and what isn't? What's prosthetic? What's motion-captured? What's green screen? It's by far been the most challenging and most satisfying movie I've ever worked on," Isis says.

TOP: *Sketch for the kids' coronation robes.*

RIGHT CENTER: *Detailing for Susan's and Lucy's crowns.*

RIGHT: *Susan in costume.*

Putting the costumes together was no easy feat either. Crucial to the process was head draper and cutter Judy Newland. Isis convinced her to take a hiatus from her regular job as head draper at the world-renowned Metropolitan Opera in New York. That was the high artistic standard Isis strived for in every area of the wardrobe department. And she got it.

Take the crowns from the coronation scene, for example. "All the flowers on Lucy's and Susan's crowns are made by our jeweler and hand-carved from shells in New Zealand. William had probably sixty-five individual pieces of jewelry, like little acorns and leaves, carefully made by hand and then plated to the crown. In this movie everything is symbolic, nothing is just 'kind of' put on anything."

There was also the small task of getting the actors into the costumes. "We hand-stitched Tilda into her costume," Isis says. "You'd go three-sixty around her and you wouldn't know how she got in the dress or how she'd get out."

The kids had plenty of changes, too. Skandar was by far the hardest to fit, "because he never stood still for three seconds," Isis remembers. "But when sweet Anna put on her coronation dress for the first time, she let loose and twirled with delight. The girls were so happy to be in dresses after tromping around in their first outfits for so long. A special day sticks out in her mind, when Georgie first tried on her fancy coronation dress. Her mother, Helen,

TOP: Edmund on the throne.

ABOVE: Lucy in her dress.

offered to bring her in at the end of a long, tired day of shooting so we could fit her. So they came into my office at the end of the day; everybody's madly working in the workroom. We put this dress on her; you can see it's not even done. It's pinned here and there and we put on her beautiful crown for the first time, with all the beading and all the ribbon work. She just about fainted, she was so pleased. She said, 'This is the most beautiful thing I've ever put on in my life.' All of a sudden this tired little girl just started beaming. Thirty-five people in our department were in the room and Georgie turned around to all of us and said, 'Thank you so much, everybody, for my beautiful dress. It makes me feel like a princess and I've never worn anything so beautiful.' It was the greatest gift."

WHAT IT ALL MEANS: AN INTERVIEW WITH DOUGLAS GRESHAM, C. S. LEWIS'S STEPSON

On a rainy day on the Hobsonville Air Force base soundstage, I took Doug Gresham to our beautiful set for the train station in the opening scene. The period set was empty except for a small camera crew and our unit publicist, Ernie Malik, a supremely dedicated and talented Narnia fan if there ever was one.

It was the perfect occasion for a chat with Doug. I left Doug with Ernie, and the two found out they had much to talk about. When I came back a few hours later, they were still talking, and it seemed as if they'd touched only the tip of the iceberg. No one can give you a window into the world of C. S. Lewis quite like Doug, the great protector of his work.

— Perry Moore

ERNIE: *What's your connection to this project?*

DOUG: That was summed up rather well by Perry, who introduced me to the young lass who's playing Susan by saying, "This is all his fault" [*laughs*]. I've wanted to see a movie made of *The Lion, the Witch and the Wardrobe* for probably twenty-five or thirty years. I've been working on getting it done for almost twenty years, been intensely involved with chasing it up for about the last ten or so years as the creative and artistic director of the C. S.

LEFT: *Doug looks at a location.*

ABOVE: *Doug as a child (on right) with C. S. Lewis and his brother at the old Lewis home.*

Lewis Company, and been involved with this incarnation since it started.

As C. S. Lewis's stepson, I suppose it's fair to say that I'm the only man in the world who grew up, in a sense, in Narnia, because I grew up with Jack as my stepfather. I was introduced at a very young age to *The Chronicles of Narnia* as they were written and published. *The Lion, the Witch and the Wardrobe*, which was first published in 1950, was probably my favorite book in all the world. I learned to read quite early, and I was

man who was on speaking terms with King Peter of Narnia and Aslan, the great Lion. As an eight-year-old boy, I expected him to be wearing silver armor and carrying a sword. Of course, he was nothing like that at all. He was a stooped, balding, professorial gentleman with scruffy clothes and nicotine-stained fingers. His brother, Warnie, was equally strange to me. These were English people, and I'd only just arrived in England. So initially I was a bit disappointed. But Jack's vibrant personality, his compassion, his warmth, his enormous humor soon overrode any visual discrepancies in my mind.

ERNIE: *Did he ever read to you from the Narnia books?*

DOUG: He read passages to me at times, particularly when he was working on a new book. He had a wonderful reading voice, though his accent and intonation would sound very affected to today's ears. It was very much an academic Oxford accent.

ERNIE: *The experience must've been almost unbelievable to you as a young boy.*

DOUG: Looking back on it, of course, it was an enormous privilege to grow up with Jack as a stepfather. It was an enormous privilege to live in that household. But at the time it happened, it was just the way things were. When you're a kid, this is your life; you just accept it. So I never thought it was strange to be hearing little hints about Narnia. But sometimes we'd talk at the dinner table about Narnian Dwarfs and what they liked and what they didn't like, and Jack would occasionally mention what the characters were doing. As a result, I probably know more about Narnia than any other living human being [*laughs*].

reading for myself by the time the rest of them began to be published. I absolutely adored them. Still do.

ERNIE: *Tell me about the first time you met Jack. You had an expectation. . . .*

DOUG: The problem was, I was a little American kid, brought up in upstate New York. I'd read and loved *The Lion, the Witch and the Wardrobe*. And here I was, straight out of America, going to meet the

---

ABOVE: *Sketch of Cair Paravel.*

BELOW: *The Inklings.*

OPPOSITE: *C. S. Lewis writing at his desk.*

ERNIE: *Well, that's why we have you talking here! Another privilege you had was attending the Inklings gatherings.* [Author's Note: The Inklings was a spirited fellowship of English enthusiasts and scholars who met weekly at a pub to discuss their work and exchange ideas. Notable members included renowned fantasy authors C. S. Lewis, J. R. R. Tolkien, and Charles Williams.]

DOUG: Yes, two or three times Jack took me along, probably when there was no one available to look after me. It was probably a bit of a chore to him, actually. But I was only a child; I think the oldest I was when I went to an Inklings get-together was probably twelve or fourteen, maybe fifteen. The Inklings were an extraordinary group of men with immensely powerful minds. There's a kind of a strange attitude in the academic circles of today that great minds have to be dour, serious. In fact, the reverse was true of these men: they had huge senses of humor, and the repartee and the wit and the flow of their conversation was amazing. The hallmark of an Inklings meeting, and I remember it well, was laughter. I would be given my half-pint of beer; then I'd sit in one corner and look on. I was amazed at the humor, the huge roars of laughter that kept coming from these men. They had a great time together. That was one of the significant things about Jack's personality that gets lost in all of the biographies about him. Although he was a Christian man and therefore conscious of his own sinfulness, he was equally conscious of his own salvation, and he rejoiced in it. He was a man of immense humor. You couldn't be in a room with Jack for ten minutes without starting to laugh. Even in the dark, painful, troubled times of my mother's illness, the humor never failed him. It never failed her, either.

ERNIE: *Growing up with him, do you remember how his books were received by critics and colleagues?*

DOUG: I knew a lot of the people in Oxford at the time resented Jack for several reasons. One

was his enormous intelligence. If you were an intellectual and you challenged Jack to a battle of wits, you'd better make damn sure you had the ammunition with which to fight. He was also resented for his success, not only in his own field, as a Fellow of English, but as a writer of children's books. To some people at the time, it was probably regarded as being a bit beneath a professor to write silly stories for children. Furthermore, he was resented quite largely for his Christian beliefs, and the fact that he was not only Christian, but visibly and muscularly so.

ERNIE: *How do you think the two world wars affected his writing?*

DOUG: I think it would be impossible for any writer to live through the kind of experiences that Jack did, particularly in the First World War, without those experiences coloring everything he wrote. The First World War is unique in the history of mankind. Up until that point, soldiers had journeyed to the battlefield, fought the battle, and then gone elsewhere. In the First World War, you went to the battlefield, and there you lived, and fought, and died. Not just day by day, but week by week, month by month, and for some people, year by year. That sort of experience cannot help but leave horrendous scars on a man's soul.

Jack learned that there's no glory in war. There's glory in some of the deeds performed in war, but war itself is a hideous business. He also learned that it doesn't matter what social class you come from: you have every bit as good a chance of being a good bloke or a bad bloke as the next fellow. Jack also learned an awful lot about fear, and how to deal with it and how it affects you. That comes through quite strongly in the Narnia Chronicles. Fear not merely for oneself, but for one's loved ones. Jack and his brother both found themselves more tormented by fear for each other's safety than by fear for their own. And that comes out in the Narnia books.

ERNIE: *Where did the name Narnia come from?*

DOUG: There's a school of thought that holds that Jack, in his reading of the great classics of Roman literature, must have come across the town in Italy called Narni, which in Roman times was called Narnia, and adapted it to his own use. There's someone who claims that Jack told him this, but I don't know. It's just as possible that Jack made the name up. He was quite capable of inventing his own nomenclature, and often did, in other books.

ERNIE: *And the other myth we can debunk is the wardrobe that sits in the Wade Center at Wheaton College, Illinois.*

DOUG: Well, there are two wardrobes, actually, in different universities in America. The wardrobe that used to be in the hall at The Kilns, the old Lewis home — a beautiful piece of furniture, handmade by Jack's grandfather of black oak — is now in the Wade Center. I'm very glad for them to have it, because they're lovely people there, but it's not the wardrobe that inspired the wardrobe in *The Lion, the Witch and the Wardrobe*. The one in the book is described as having mirrors in its door, and this one doesn't have mirrors. And there's another wardrobe at another university somewhere else—I apologize that I can't remember the name of that university and where it is—which stood in Warnie's bedroom at The Kilns. But *every* bedroom in that house had a wardrobe. There was no actual "*the* wardrobe"; it was a literary device to get children from one world to another.

ERNIE: *What was the inspiration for Aslan the Lion? Did you ever talk to Jack about that?*

DOUG: When Jack was about sixteen, the image came into his head of a Faun in a snowy wood carrying parcels with an umbrella. He never did anything with it until he was about fifty, when he decided to try to make a story out of the scene. At the time, he was having a lot of dreams about lions for some reason. And suddenly, as Jack put it himself, Aslan leaped into his mind and into the story and dragged all the rest of *The Chronicles of Narnia* with him. But the rational way he arrived at a lion for this particular role, if you like to put it that way, was because he wanted to write a suppositional representation of what it might be like if there really were a world where animals spoke and thought cogently. And if God had to in some way save that world from evil, just as he had to save this one, how might he have gone about it and what might have happened?

ERNIE: *And his inspiration for Jadis, the White Witch?*

DOUG: Jadis. Now that's a difficult one. She represents, first of all, the enemy himself, the devil, in a way. But she also represents one of the devil's techniques. If you remember, she was startlingly beautiful. That represents, I believe, the character and nature of Satan's favorite temptations. The devil isn't stupid; he's not going to try to tempt us with something that's ugly. One of the mistakes that most horror filmmakers and horror writers make is to make all of the devil's temptations appear as ugly things. The devil dresses up his temptations in beauty, more often than not.

Doug Gresham and Tilda Swinton discuss the White Witch's origins on her "rack of pain."

ERNIE: *Would you repeat the anecdote about the person who inspired the character of Lucy? She's an actress now, right?*

DOUG: Indeed she is. When Jack and Warnie were living at The Kilns in the Second World War, various children were evacuated from London to them. One in particular stood out, a girl who came originally as an evacuee, then came back of her own choice, sacrificing at the time something she dearly wanted to do in order to help the people at The Kilns—Jack, Warnie, Mrs. Moore, and so on—to be of assistance to them. She was described by Jack and Warnie as the closest person they'd ever met to a living saint, the embodiment of Christian principles and virtue in one human being. Many years later I was talking with Warnie about *The Lion, the Witch and the Wardrobe,* and he told me that Lucy was based on Jill Flewett, this girl who'd been with them at The Kilns. Later on she became an actress in her own right.

ERNIE: *Since Jack starts the story in the year 1900, was the series of books intended to be a comment on the twentieth century?*

DOUG: I don't think so at all, except that, if you're writing in the twentieth century, no matter what you write, it will be a comment on the twentieth century. You can't avoid that. Even if you write a piece set in ancient Rome and you do your very best to reflect ancient Rome as it was at the time, you're still reflecting it from the eyes of a present-day thinker.

Jack wrote the Narnia Chronicles for many reasons, but one of the most important ones was that he and Tolkien thought no one of their era

was writing children's books that they themselves, when they were children, would have wanted to read, and no one was writing children's books as they ought to be written. So they decided to do it themselves. So in one sense the Narnia Chronicles aren't so much a commentary on the twentieth century as they are a reaction to it. Jack wanted to lead children in the right direction, stimulating their imagination and giving them important truths to deal with. He wanted to offer them hope, and truth, and joy.

ERNIE: *Were these books written just for children? Or for people of all ages?*

DOUG: Jack did write these books for children. But his theory was that if a book is worth reading when you're five, it's equally worth reading when you're fifty. If you can't reread it at the age of fifty and get as much out of it as you did at the age of five, then you shouldn't have read it when you were five anyway. So *The Chronicles of Narnia* are to be read to children, to be read by children, and to be read by adults with great joy even to the last days of their lives.

Andrew consulting with the C. S. Lewis Estate.

ERNIE: *How has your interpretation and appreciation of the books changed from the time you were five years old? You mentioned you continue to read them.*

DOUG: I read them all the time. I don't interpret them. I think that's a mistake a lot of people make: trying to interpret what they read. Read a book for its own sake. Let the book work its interpretation on you. Don't try to mold the book to meet your ideas; let the ideas of the book mold you, if you're reading something good. And if you're not reading something good, read something else!

ERNIE: *Do the books serve to introduce children to Greek mythology? This particular book seems to be quite influenced by it. You might disagree.*

DOUG: No, I agree with you. But I think it's more a matter of stimulating the imagination, so that when children meet Greek mythology later, they have something to relate it to. Jack loved the Greek mythological creatures and characters so dearly that he wanted to have them in his own fiction. This is one of the things that Tolkien didn't like about the Narnia Chronicles, because he was something of a mythical purist. He liked his myths kept as myths, and he didn't like to take characters out of them and put them in somewhere else. He didn't like Jack's playing with these characters the way he did.

ERNIE: *You said it's taken a couple of decades to get to this point.*

DOUG: Today we finally have the technology to do this series of books justice. Previous attempts simply didn't. And on this particular project not only do we have the technology, we also have one of the world's leading masters of the art of computer-generated imagery in director Andrew Adamson. So now is the time, and here is the place. I've been thrilled at what I've seen here. I think this movie is probably going to be the beginning of a new genre of filmmaking. This is going to be a superb motion picture.

ERNIE: *What are your thoughts on the casting?*

DOUG: We've got a brilliant cast. And it's interesting, these four children playing siblings in rehearsals and on-screen are developing actual sibling relationships. They're becoming a family. And they're great kids. If these had been my children or grandchildren, I'd have been as proud of them as I'm sure their parents are, as proud of them as I am of my own family. They're all sensitive, intelligent, funny children, and they're good actors and actresses.

ERNIE: *What did you and Andrew talk about the first time you met?*

DOUG: Well, I told him that if we ever made *The Silver Chair*, I would want him to play Puddleglum [*laughs*]. Besides that, though, we were feeling each other out, obviously. All I knew about Andrew was that he'd done *Shrek*, which was entirely computer-generated. The only tiny question mark hanging over Andrew's head as a director for me was whether he could handle the mobs of extras that you need on a live location, on a live set, among the live actors. It turns out I needn't have worried: the guy is a genius. And he's so gentle and sensitive in the way he works that the cast and crew want to do the best they can for him. And that's the hallmark, in my mind, of a great director, not just a good one, but a *great* director. And I hope he blushes when he hears this. He is, to my mind, the only man to do the job today.

ERNIE: *Andrew is quoted as saying this movie will become a classic in its medium.*

DOUG: It's a thrilling picture. It's immensely powerful, and it will remain in people's minds for a long, long time.

ERNIE: *These books seem to have a nineteenth-century influence on them. How do Disney and Walden Media adapt them to a twenty-first-century audience?*

DOUG: I don't think you have to do anything except stick to the book. Be as faithful as possible

Andrew as Puddleglum?

to the original book, and it'll do it for you. The story is so classic, so true, so honest, so straightforward, that the less we mess around with it, the better off we'll be.

ERNIE: *Do you have a favorite passage from* **The Lion, the Witch and the Wardrobe?**

DOUG: Yes. It comes from the scene where the children first meet Aslan in Narnia:

"Welcome, Peter, son of Adam," said Aslan. "Welcome, Susan and Lucy, daughters of Eve. Welcome, He-Beaver and She-Beaver." His voice was deep and rich, and somehow it took the fidgets out of them. They now felt glad and quiet, and it didn't seem awkward to them to stand and say nothing. "But where is the fourth?" asked Aslan. "He has tried to betray them and join the White Witch, O Aslan," said Mr. Beaver. And then something made Peter say, "That was partly my fault, Aslan. I was angry with him and I think that helped him to go wrong." And Aslan said nothing either to excuse Peter or to blame him, but merely stood looking at him with his great golden eyes. And it seemed to all of them that there was nothing to be said. "Please, Aslan," said Lucy, "can anything be done to save Edmund?" "All shall be done," said Aslan. "But it may be harder than you think."

ERNIE: *Why that particular passage?*

DOUG: Because to me it sums up the whole book. Aslan is saying, Yes, I know. I know the grief you're feeling. I know the fear you're feeling. And I will help. But it's going to be tough. It's going to take sacrifice, self-discipline, and pain. But it will be done.

ERNIE: *And we are done. Thank you very much.*

DOUG: My pleasure.

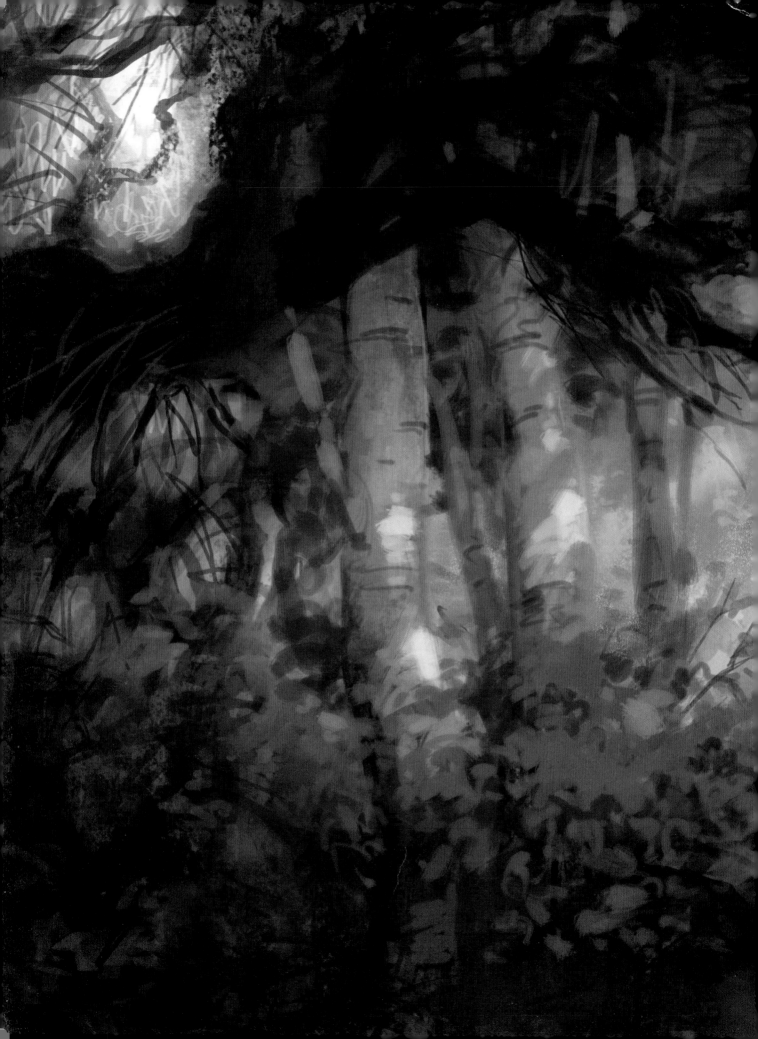

CREDITS

Photographs

PHIL BRAY: vi-vii, xii, xiii, 5, 8, 9, 14-15, 15 (bottom), 16-17, 20, 22, 23, 24, 25, 30, 31, 34, 35 (bottom), 36, 37, 38-39, 40, 41, 42, 43, 44, 48, 50 (bottom), 52, 53, 54-55, 56, 57, 58, 59, 60, 66 (top), 67, 68-69, 70-71, 72, 73, 74-75, 80, 81, 82, 84-85, 87, 88-89, 90, 91, 92, 93, 96, 97, 98, 99, 100-101, 102-103, 109, 110, 111, 112, 113 (bottom), 118, 120, 121, 122-123, 128-129, 130, 131, 133 (top), 134, 136, 137, 138-139, 140, 141, 142-143, 145, 150-151, 152, 159, 160 (bottom), 161, 162, 164-165, 169, 170, 171, 178, 180-181, 182, 184, 185, 186-187, 188, 189, 191, 192-193, 195, 196, 197, 198, 200, 206, 207, 208 (bottom), 209, 210, 216, 219, 222

LARRY HORRICKS: 8 (bottom), 18-19, 198

PHOTOS COLLECTED BY PERRY MOORE AND USED BY PERMISSION OF THEIR OWNERS: xi (KEYNES), 15 (top), 16, 22 (top), 24 (far left), 26-27 (HALL), 35 (top, POPPLEWELL), 46 (top, HALL), 46 (bottom, POPPLEWELL), 49, 51, 61, 64, 65, 66 (bottom), 79 (HENLEY), 83 (HENLEY), 86 (POPPLEWELL), 92, 106 (bottom, GRESHAM), 113 (top, POPPLEWELL), 114, 115 (SAROFIM), 116 (HENLEY), 117, 118 (POPPLEWELL), 119, 123 (CHAPLA), 133, 133 (bottom, POPPLEWELL), 144 (bottom), 160 (top), 168 (bottom), 172 (BERGER), 173 (BERGER), 174-175 (BERGER), 179, 183 (WRIGHT), 189 (bottom, POPPLEWELL), 194 (WRIGHT), 201, 204 (bottom, WARDROBE), 218, 223 (SLAB)

PIERRE VINET: iii, v, 28-29, 32, 33, 45 (bottom left), 47, 50 (top), 61 (left), 62-63, 76, 77, 78, 104, 105, 106 (top), 107, 108, 126, 127, 149, 202-203, 204, 225

WADE COLLECTION: 8, 211, 212, 213. Used by permission of the The Marion E. Wade Collection, Wheaton College, Wheaton, Illinois.

Illustrations

HOPE ATHERTON: 91, 205, 206, 207

PAULINE BAYNES: 166, copyright © 1953 by C.S. Lewis Pte. Ltd.

JOHN HOWE: 2, 3, 154 (top)

ALAN LEE: 13

RPIN SUWANNATH: 22-23, 164-165, 190

JUSTIN SWEET: viii, 6-7, 154 (bottom two)

HENRIK TAMM: 10-11, 12, 21, 94-95, 146-147, 154-155, 176-177, 212, 214-215, 220-221

GYPSY TAYLOR: 45, 61, 77, 208

WETA: 4, 59, 80, 132, 153, 156, 157, 158, 168, 196, 217

Narnian weapons and armor as authentic as any of genuine Dwarf make and people crafting the weird and ghastly creatures of evil that follow the White Witch. I have watched forested landscapes being built by hand, and then dressed with fine snow; a Faun's cave taking shape beneath the hands of skilled craftsmen, a Beaver's dam house, and a strange and eerie fortress of ice.

And then there have been those whose canvas has been the faces of our wonderful actors whose work is of such importance, the makeup people responsible for changing the whole appearance of our cast to better enable them to convey what is happening within their characters. I felt for cast members inside prosthetic costumes, sweltering in the sun, their "minders," between takes, blowing air with little battery-powered electric fans into the heads of their creature costumes to allow them to breathe. And I was grateful for the caterers who kept us all sustained throughout the filming, the transport coordinators and their drivers who kept us mobile, and to all of those who labored invisibly and unknown to keep our mobile towns functioning as they moved from location to location and into and out of soundstages here and there. I have met scores of fascinating and friendly people all around the world, made new friends, and found both saints and sinners amongst them. The making of a hugely complex movie like this one is a microcosm of life itself and the people who brought it about are without doubt a wonderful bunch.

So many amazing places and so many wonderful people; how do you thank those who have made your dream come true? It can't really be done and yet I feel compelled to try. How can one convey what it means to a father to see his businessman son deeply moved on a film location set and on enquiring what was troubling him to be told that all his life as long as he can remember he has heard me dreaming, talking, scheming, and planning how someday I would make a movie of *The Lion, the Witch and the Wardrobe,* and now he suddenly found it happening all around him? How can I express how I felt when my grown-up daughter was suddenly moved almost to tears as she walked through Aslan's battle camp, and who said that all her life, since she was a little girl, she had always, way back in the dark recesses of her mind, harbored and nurtured the gentle belief that somewhere, somehow, Narnia was real, and now here she was walking in the middle of it? Or the time when my visiting three-year-old granddaughter was growing tired and Andrew told us to let her rest on Lucy's bed on the set, and she fell fast asleep all unheeding while the movie grew around her? How can I possibly convey in words how moments like those, along with hundreds of others, are so treasured in my mind? I can't, it is a task beyond my meager talents. All I can do is to say "thank you" to everyone who, in every way from the greatest to the least, contributed to this film being made.

Now it is done, and now we all hand it over to you and invite you to come for a short while and join us where we have had the enormous good fortune to spend the past several years of our lives—in Narnia.

Blessings,
Douglas Gresham.
Ireland, June 2005

A DREAM
COMES TRUE

An Afterword by Douglas Gresham

NOW THE MAGIC BEGINS. WE HAVE MADE a movie. Not without trials and difficulties, too numerous to discuss, not without tears, blood, and toil, but withal and through all the whole project has been suffused with love. I am not talking about some slushy romanticism, but a great power of unity that seemed to pervade the entire crew and cast of this immense project. I have dreamed and schemed about making this film almost all of my adult life and indeed even back in my teen years, and now I have watched this lifelong dream come true before my eyes— a privilege afforded to very few.

The making of this film has been an amazing experience for many reasons and in many ways. First is the simple fact of it happening at all, but over and above that is the fact that now, this particular moment in the history of Man, is absolutely the right time to make this film. A few short years ago the technology to really do justice to the work simply did not exist, today it does. Not long ago the whole genre of "Beauty Fantasy" in movies was almost out of fashion. Today it is coming back into fashion with a vengeance. It is my feeling that all the right people for this project were on this project,

and for that to happen takes such an amazing collection of collaborating forces that it had to be miraculous.

For me, journeying to New Zealand and the Czech Republic for filming, to America and England for numerous meetings, has been a rich and varied experience. It is my view that when one stops learning one starts dying. This whole journey from that first meeting in New York between Melvin Adams and Perry Moore, to today when I sit in my office and write this addendum to Perry's book about how the movie was made, has been a fascinating and exciting learning experience.

I have been so privileged as to watch many hours of work being performed by masters of their various crafts. Artists devising sets and crafting models of them before they are constructed life-size on the various soundstages, carpenters and woodworkers building the sets, painters painting them with amazing skill, astonishing artisans crafting realistic waterfalls and cliffs of ice or stone from all sorts of synthetic materials, costume artists creating wondrous outfits of strange materials and also 1940s clothing. I saw swordsmiths creating coverage. When the clouds drifted back, Andrew worked with the girls, and a few takes later that was it. "Check the gate," he said after the shot. It was the last time we'd hear that phrase in New Zealand. Then there were cheers, and everyone ran out into the final shot for one last group picture. Andrew ordered a martini bar brought out in the mud, and we all toasted the shoot.

Andrew pulled each of the children aside separately and congratulated them. He'd been a huge part of their lives for such a long time, and he loved each of those kids. He first reached out and hugged Anna, whispering something in her ear. She broke into tears through a broad smile. She'd been telling everyone that everything was going to be fine to steel herself against the emotional tug of leaving something so special behind, and here it all came flooding out. Will ran over and wrapped his arms around her as Anna laughed through her tears.

Of course, there was still so much to do: the remaining shots in the Czech Republic, the visual effects, the editing, the score, the mass-marketing and publicity . . . the sequel. No rest for the wicked. Still, this was a major milestone in this movie's history, and we all took a moment to enjoy it.

A reel of outtakes played at the wrap party, and all of us laughed at the long, strange trip we'd taken. Andrew hopped up on a table and

A final sunset.

gave a moving speech, short but heartfelt. Plenty of toasts followed, plenty of thank-yous, lots of good-byes. Giants and Dwarfs, script supervisors and caterers, Centaurs and Dryads, assistant directors and drivers.

Shane Rangi, General Otmin himself, gave a special Maori blessing to my carved greenstone Tiki. It was one of the highlights of the movie for me. Despite the tough conditions, there is such a strong connection to the land, and I believe that connection shines in the movie.

It's these memories that we would take with us. These bonds that we would carry around with us forever. Although we were ready to return home, ready to celebrate the holidays, ready to enjoy a hard-earned respite, we were going to miss each other. Fiercely. We had a new family now. This was the only way to make this movie, the only way to make it *right*. C. S. Lewis wouldn't have had it any other way.

"We'll always have Prague" became our mantra as we fought off the bittersweet feelings of moving on from something so special. It was a reference to the limited cast and crew who would pick up a few of the winter shots on location in Prague after the holidays. It was a nice sentiment, but there's a mantra that each of us can say that's a little more accurate: we'll always have Narnia.

WE'LL ALWAYS HAVE PRAGUE: THE FINAL DAYS OF SHOOTING

ALL GOOD THINGS MUST COME TO AN END, and so we wrapped production in New Zealand on Saturday, December 18, 2004.

The week leading up to our final days on set was fraught with adverse conditions. Our last day of shooting saw hail, sleet, freezing temperatures, and mud. On the top of the mountain, there was actually a blizzard. This was the day before the longest day of *summer* in New Zealand, and we were shivering by portable heaters trying to get the crane through the mud.

Since this was their first movie experience, Georgie and Will had been asking Anna all week if they were going to be sad when it all came to an end. They looked to Anna, the veteran, for guidance.

"It will be fine. We'll see each other all the time; there's nothing to be sad about," she said. When they protested, she admonished, "Oh,

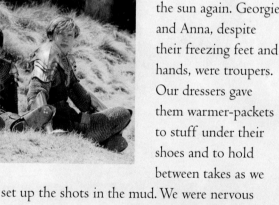

don't be silly," settling the matter perfectly sensible as Susan.

Cut to our last day, our last shot. Picking up a shot we'd missed earlier, Susan and Lucy walked Aslan through the forest on his way to the Stone Table—a somber, heartfelt scene that required overcast conditions; we waited patiently for clouds to cover the sun again. Georgie and Anna, despite their freezing feet and hands, were troupers. Our dressers gave them warmer-packets to stuff under their shoes and to hold between takes as we set up the shots in the mud. We were nervous that we weren't going to get the shot before the day was over, and the only thing worse than wondering about the end of the shoot would be to prolong it.

Andrew assured us that we'd get what we needed. He was determined. Finally some cloud